CHOOSI

Is it love or just a
hold? How can I
These questions and many, many more can be answered by various occult techniques. From biorhythms to runes, from body language to graphology, from tealeaf readings to Ouija-board predictions, these psychic paths provide insights that will help you improve your love life, better understand yourself, and find the perfect mate.

Love Games: Psychic Paths to Love explains all these methods so that you can maximize your romantic potential. Each section is tailored to answer your most intimate questions and help you solve your love-life dilemmas. You'll learn how each psychic discipline can aid you in different ways: reviving a sagging romance, finding out whether that good-looking stranger is interested, knowing what to expect from a date or a lover, and determining the best times to look for love—or to make a commitment to your partner. With so many techniques to choose from, you'll never be alone again!

NANCY FREDERICK SUSSAN is an astrologer who writes about a variety of metaphysical topics. Her articles appear frequently in every astrology magazine on the stands. The editor of ASTRO SIGNS, read daily by upwards of half a million people across North America, Ms. Sussan also writes, teaches astrology, and counsels a large private clientele.

The Love Life Guides

#1 Starring Your Love Life
#2 It All Adds Up to Love
#3 The Lover's Dream
#4 Tarot: Love is in the Cards
#5 Palmistry: All Lines Lead to Love
#6 Love Games: Psychic Paths to Love

LOVE GAMES: PSYCHIC PATHS TO LOVE

Nancy Frederick Sussan

LYNX BOOKS
New York

LOVE GAMES: PSYCHIC PATHS TO LOVE

ISBN: 1-55802-046-2

First Printing/December 1988

This book is published by Lynx Books, a division of Lynx Communications, Inc., 41 Madison Avenue, New York, New York, 10010. The name ''Lynx'' together with the logotype consisting of a stylized head of a lynx is a trademark of Lynx Communications, Inc.

Printed in the United States of America

0 9 8 7 6 5 4 3 2 1

contents

LOVE GAMES: PSYCHIC PATHS TO LOVE

CHAPTER I

Introduction

WHAT DOES YOUR FUTURE HOLD? WILL YOU meet your true love and settle down to a lifetime of bliss, or will you keep searching patiently for the one soul mate who will complete you unalterably? These are the questions that untold millions of people have asked since the beginning of time. We all seek answers to the all-important issues of love, marriage, success, and happiness.

The occult offers many paths to insight. There are many areas of the occult, and all endeavor to find the truth about you, your life, and the personal questions that matter so deeply to you. The interesting thing about the occult is that no matter what path you take, the answers will usually be similar. That's because they are your own personal and specific answers. If you go to a competent practitioner of each of the various occult arts, you are likely to receive amazingly similar information.

Thus a good astrologer will offer many of the same insights as a good numerologist or a good palmist. The astrologer's predictions are very likely to match those made by the Tarot or tea leaf reader. The rune-master will give you some of the same guidance that a Tarot reader could offer. And the graphologist will provide you with some of the same personality information that the astrologer imparts. It's amazing.

But it isn't really that astonishing, for though the occult is mysterious, each of its disciplines simply represents a different path to the truth, and there is only one real truth as far as each of us is concerned. It's up to you to find your own truth through one or several of the paths charted for you here in this book, each of which has its own specialty.

If you want deep personality information, consult the handwriting analysis section. That chapter provides all the information you need to get to know a potential mate. What is his or her love style? What can you expect in the way of practical considerations or sexual sizzle? His or her handwriting will give you essential clues that can help you prevent mistakes and be confident in your choice of the appropriate date or mate.

Deep psychological information about where you are going with your own life and how you can make it more fulfilling is contained in the runes. As you experiment with these magical stones, you will begin to feel the wisdom of the ages at your disposal. You will get a sense of higher powers communicating directly with and for you on the most deeply personal issues of your life. Then you can use that information to heighten your own expression of the universal life force. A rune message each day can become an excellent meditation tool that opens you up to your higher self and greater purpose for life and love.

Psychological information about the other guy can be obtained through body language. What are the hidden messages that your dates and friends send out? How do they really feel about you and themselves? Are you headed for heartbreak or true love? Such questions are answered by body language, something far easier to translate than Latin! You can spot those seeking intimacy and openness and those who are too guarded to do so. It's your chance to peek into another person's psyche and use that information in your own choice-making process when it comes to romance.

Further clues about that decision-making process are contained within biorhythms, which chart the various cycles within your own physical system. Biorhythms can show you new means of scheduling so that you can take advantage of your own best days. You'll soon begin to understand why you feel sexy and passionate on some days and private and withdrawn on others. You can achieve greater success in life and love through scheduling special events or romantic rendez-vous to coincide with the days on which you are likely to turn in a peak performance. Biorhythms are also a valid means of analyzing the compatibility of lovers on a day-by-day basis. Always at odds with your mate sexually? Your biorhythms will explain why. Some people are never on the same wavelength, and thus either a change or a compromise is in order. With the information provided by your biorhythms you can stop quarreling and start scheduling for optimum results.

Want to know what the future will bring? Check your tea leaves. This ancient art of reading the symbols that appear like little pictures in the bottom of your cup has existed for centuries. You can read your own cup or your lover's and get very accurate clues about what the future will hold for each of you. And you can take advantage of that information to plan your life and to gain confidence, because forewarned is definitely forearmed.

The Ouija board can also help you glimpse the future as it puts you in touch with the spiritual elements that surround you. With this amazing spiritual tool, you have the ability to tap into the deepest possible information, because the Ouija board allows you to communicate directly with the universal spiritual reservoir of knowledge. There is nothing, past or future, that cannot be determined. Of course, your destiny isn't written in stone, but rather it is an ever-evolving process determined by your choices in the present. And that is the probable future that the Ouija board can predict, offering you valuable insight into your present choices. That insight will enable you to change or solidify those choices and thereby alter the course of your destiny through increased awareness and an open mind.

This book offers you a wealth of information and a scope of awareness so that you can develop greater insight into your own life and the lives of those you love. And the better you know yourself and others, the greater your chances for success in romance! With this enhanced point of view you gain confidence and power, for you realize that your fate is not beyond your control, but solidly within your own grasp. You have the power both to create your life and to change it, and all the information provided here will aid you in the process. Knowing your options and the life that you have created as a result of your choices gives you a sense of yourself and forms the map of your destiny. Upon examination you will see where you have been and where that has led you today. From these you can project where you will be going tomorrow. And that information gives you the chance to stop and examine the meaning of it all. What does your life stand for? On what foundation have you formed yourself? With this information you can rule your own world, because you have created the life you currently lead and you have the power to change that life for the better if you so choose.

Take charge of your own life. Forge your own destiny along the most joyous lines possible. Open yourself up to life, to love, to true happiness. You can have success, prosperity, and true love with the soul mate of your dreams. All it takes is awareness and a spirit that believes it is possible. Great joy can be yours—if you choose. Choose happiness. Choose love. Make your life wonderful, and the rest of the world will rejoice for you.

CHAPTER II

handwriting analysis

AFTER HER DIVORCE SOME YEARS AGO, AND before it was a widely accepted practice, Jenna decided to try something she considered quite risqué: She answered some ads in the personals. She had great success with her letters, receiving a call for almost every ad she answered. Jenna thought that her high rate of reply was due to her writing ability and humor, but she found out differently when several of the guys she met confided to her that they had responded so readily because of her handwriting. One said that it was so neat, precise, and pretty that it just seemed sexy. As Jenna thought about it, she realized that the qualities describing her handwriting also described her, and she began to wonder if perhaps she was sending out a subliminal message through the handwriting itself. Her curiosity was piqued, and so she decided to study graphology, or handwriting analysis. After all, perhaps she would place an ad herself someday, and through the graphology techniques she would learn, Jenna would have a better chance of correctly evaluating her potential dates.

You can do the same thing, whether you plan to analyze the handwriting of strangers or of people you already know. Of the various psychic arts, handwriting analysis is one of the few disciplines that is accepted in business and industry. So accurate and respected is this science that many top-notch organizations employ graphologists to screen applicants for new and higher-level positions. Whatever your purpose in learning graphology, it can serve you well—and it's a lot of fun!

The first step is to look at a writing sample. This is one case in which you certainly can judge a book by its cover. Take your time in examining the sample. What initial impression have you formed as a result of looking at it? Just as you might form a reasonable judgment upon a first meeting—if you are introduced to a man who is wearing an unironed shirt, a stained tie, and rumpled pants, you would logically conclude that he is a slob—in a similar way you can form a reasonably accurate first impression from looking at a bit of handwritten text.

What do you notice first? One important consideration is the general energy level communicated by the writer. Does the sample look energetic? Do the letters flow across the page with speed and determination? If so, you can logically conclude that this is an individual with a good degree of vitality, someone who is action oriented and aggressive. Such a lover will be an asset, because he or she is determined to make a mark on the world, and on your life. He or she will be vigorous and exciting, someone who'll be there to share many good times. This mate will pitch in and contribute his or her fair share of the energy needed for any task. And when it comes to sex, vitality is essential. Who wants a lover who doesn't have the energy to pick up a pen, much less pucker? High-energy writers are also high-energy lovers, with sexual sparkle and the ability to keep on making love until both parties are satisfied. Of course, vitality in no way shows the inclination to please—only the energy to do so should the will be present.

Suppose the writing looks slow, hesitant, halting, almost as if it is laboring to get across the page? Then this person is likely to be a far less dynamic mate and certainly a less passionate lover. Such handwriting is one indication of a person who lacks confidence, who feels that, for whatever reason, the universe is not supporting his or her efforts. This mate may not be willing or able to pursue you, or even to respond passionately if you decide to be the aggressive one. Of course, if you are a super dynamo, one who likes to be the aggressor and who prefers a much weaker partner whom you can dominate, then such a mate may be your ideal. Be careful, however, to consider why it is that you feel as you do, for a constant desire to dominate is not a good or healthy sign. It could indicate a hidden source of insecurity or self-doubt.

Good pressure is another sign of vitality. You can discern the pressure by looking at the back of the page. If there is a visible imprint through the page, the writer is aggressive, strong, and determined. Such a lover will not hesitate either to respond or to make overtures to you, and he or she will be reasonably secure of a personal potential to succeed and to make a mark on the world. Remember, however, that you cannot determine pressure with the popular felt-tip pens in use today, for they require none. A ballpoint pen is a much better choice for a writing sample.

Another thing to take into account is the regularity of the hand. Does it look even, steady, and reliable? Are the spaces fairly regular, the same letters written in the same way? Such even, clean-looking writing is a sign of an emotionally secure and well-adjusted individual. He or she is confident, serene, and able to take whatever life hands out without going crazy. This lover is strong enough to continue in his or her own direction and will usually be able to survive any crisis. Obviously this is an important criterion in choosing a romantic partner. Who wants to date a psychopath, or someone who falls apart when problems arise? That could be the exact indication of very irregular, uneven writing, though those are rather extreme examples. In any event, a writing sample containing words which ramble over the page along with eccentrically formed and irregularly spaced letters can be an indication of an individual who is not emotionally stable. This partner may not be able to connect easily with a mate in a positive way that employs equal give-and-take and a good degree of affection and commitment. Extremely chaotic-looking writing is a strong indicator of a chaotic personality. Beware!

The next step is to examine the use of space within the writing sample. A page or two is ideal for a sample, because if you are trying to make conjectures based on a check or a postcard, you may have a hard time using all the criteria. Assuming that your sample is not a hastily scrawled message in limited space—such as a postcard or one of those post-it notes—the following rules apply. Also remember to use unlined paper so that your victim can control the space completely.

First look at the margins. The left margin is a sign of breeding, education, conscious effort, and organization. Every writer consciously chooses a left margin when he or she first sets pen to paper. Most of us have been taught to leave an inch or more on the left side, and usually we do follow that rule. A left-hand margin that conforms to that basic guideline indicates someone who is aware of the rules of communication, someone who will take pains to express him or herself in a way that others can easily comprehend. This is a good sign if you are considering a romance with this person, for communication is the most essential facet of any relationship. Even with great sex, couples who can't communicate adequately will eventually break up.

A narrow left-hand margin is a sign that the writer wishes to remain closed in, to protect him or herself from prying eyes. Such a person might be secretive and potentially hostile about opening up to others. Perhaps he or she has been betrayed in the past by family members or a lover and now feels guarded or hesitant about relationships. Or he or she may simply not be very communicative—such as a businesslike person who doesn't regard the social niceties as important. Or maybe the subject is just shy.

If you are dating such a person and you consider good manners as essential, then you could have a problem. He may not open the door for you, or she may light up a cigarette before you're finished with your meal. Of course these are not the worst crimes imaginable, but they are an important sign that this mate might not bother to consider your feelings. That could mean that much larger liberties will be taken, causing you to feel disappointed and frustrated. But keep in mind that if the writing sample is on a small page, such as a postcard, then the writer may simply have a lot to say and too little space in which to say it.

The left-hand margin can also begin one way and end another, if the writer lets his words drift along the page unevenly. If the left-hand margin starts out quite wide and becomes narrow toward the bottom of the page, then the writer has unconsciously chosen to become more guarded as the message goes on. This could indicate someone who has a naturally open personality but who has experienced recent pain from which he or she feels the need to be protected. Perhaps the subject matter of the writing sample has changed, becoming more sensitive, something that requires a closed-in audience. (Few professional graphologists actually *read* their samples, preferring instead to look at them for specific indications. For your purposes, though, you should read what you're analyzing, because the contents of the sample can be quite a potent source of information.) On the whole, though, someone who habitually starts out with a wide left-hand margin and then drifts to a narrow one is afraid of revealing the inner landscape. This person may be so determined to control his or her impulses that he or she will be very reticent about opening up to you on any level. Thus it could take a long period of dating and many conversations before you really know your partner. That doesn't mean that you won't have fun or won't be able to communicate. You just may have to be patient about receiving intimate information and personal confidences.

The left-hand margin can also start quite narrow and

gradually drift toward a much wider shape. Here we have the opposite personality. Such an individual is calm or reserved initially, but then becomes overtaken by his or her own enthusiasm. It is easy for a person like this to get carried away. That means that you might discover your mate is quite suggestible—not only by yourself but by every traveling salesman around. This person does well on short-term projects but may get sidetracked rather easily. If you are a seriously disciplined person, you might not enjoy such a partner, because you would feel that you can't count on him or her. On the other hand, perhaps you are *too* stodgy and disciplined and you need a bit of lightening up. In that case, such a mate could be just the ticket. Often spur-of-the-moment activity can be the most fun, and this is one partner who enjoys being spontaneous.

The right-hand margin is more of an unconscious indicator. It shows the way an individual throws himself into life and what he or she perceives as life's responses in return. Just like the left-hand margin, the right-hand margin is supposed to be an inch to an inch-and-a-half in width, but it is much more likely that it will be smaller as the writer gets carried away with the words and gets caught up with the flow of the ideas that he or she is expressing. Thus a wide right-hand margin is a strong indicator of someone who holds back, who has decided that he or she must keep a reasonable distance from others. Such a mate could be shy, standoffish, or insecure. He or she certainly won't be as sociable and friendly as the lover with a narrow right-hand margin. Wide margins are a psychological barrier to closeness, and even if you do fall in love with such a person, it is very likely that you will sense a loss of intimacy—unless you yourself are afraid of intimacy and would therefore prefer a partner who allows you your space. If this is so, it might be a good idea for both of you to confront this issue, whether it is caused by a fear of rejection, a fear of abandonment, or a fear of sex that is preventing you from opening up and revealing your inner nature to your close friends or lovers. (Naturally we're not suggesting that you should reveal yourself intimately to everyone.)

A narrow right-hand margin is a good sign that the person in question is strong and aggressive. He or she reaches out to others uninhibitedly. Such a person is aggressive, passionate, and enthusiastic, and might very well sweep you off your feet both romantically and sexually. This mate knows what he or she wants and is unashamed and doesn't hesitate to reach for it. That also means that this partner would very likely be willing to discuss personal issues in your relationship and to communicate openly with the intention of improving the relationship and both partners' happiness. That's a positive sign for the maintenance of any tie, since every worthwhile relationship requires lots of hard work and cooperation. Of course, it is important to note that with other contributing factors such a lover may also need lots of stimulus and excitement and may therefore eschew commitment in favor of a freelance status. And he or she will have the lively, attractive personality necessary to make such multiple liaisons possible.

A right-hand margin that starts out narrow and becomes wider indicates an individual whose enthusiasm for life has been quashed, either temporarily or permanently, depending on whether the condition continues. Such a person was initially open and enthusiastic about life, but due to a trauma—such as a broken heart or other series of events—retreated into a fear of self-revelation. If you are involved with such a person, you may fear that he or she will not provide the support you might need in times of stress, and you're probably right—at least until your lover gets back on his or her feet.

In the opposite case in which the right-hand margin starts out wide and becomes progressively more narrow, there is an indication that the writer is developing strength and enthusiasm, perhaps for the subject matter of the paragraph, or possibly for life itself. This could be someone who was very shy as a child, but who is developing greater strength and courage through personal determination. Such a lover can be inspiring, because he or she might have triumphed over severe obstacles and such an example can be encouraging to us all. You'll enjoy spending time with this lover because he or she probably has a great deal of empathy and insight into your emotions and personal life. On the other hand, he or she will probably always be a bit shy and thus may prefer to concentrate on you and your relationship without engaging in too much socializing with others. If you are a rather private person yourself, then this can be a welcome attitude, but if you're a social butterfly, you may feel hampered by this homebody.

The last margin to notice is the one at the bottom of the page. If the writing continues to the very bottom of the page, that is one indication that the writer is sexy and uninhibited. (There are additional considerations about sexuality that will be explored later.) Such a writer enjoys erotic activity and may be quite free in discussing sex, because he or she feels that there is nothing at all to hide. To this lover sex is natural, normal, and wonderful. He or she may have an active fantasy life and no objections at all to role-playing in the bedroom—or under the coffee table! Assuming your own sexual orientation is similar, this is a positive thing. You know what they say about nymphomaniacs—a nymphomaniac is someone who wants sex one time more than you do! So if you tend to stop well before the end of a page and feel that you are somewhat inhibited—you may refer to it as proper—then such a sexually uninhibited partner may be too much for you to handle. Sex is personal, and whatever feels right to an individual is right for that individual—no judgments necessary. Be as liberal as you want to be and find a lover who conforms to your own standards. Of course, if you are a sexual novice and are determined to gain some experience, a partner with a narrow bottom margin could provide all the tutoring you could possibly wish for!

The next spatial consideration is the distribution of the lines. Are they spread out, with acres of space between each line? Are they written practically one on top of the other? The space between lines gives you important clues to the individual's approach to life. In this case, balance is essential. A reasonable amount of space between lines is the best choice. Such a person will display good judgment, strong values, and a well-developed sense of aesthetics. This mate is a good partner because he or she puts a lot of thought into every action, as if each decision is an expression of personal identity. He or she is a strong, confident, thinking and feeling individual. He or she is capable and skillful and will be good at maneuvering through life successfully. Obviously you would want such a person by your side for help, support, and camaraderie.

Someone who leaves lots of extra space between lines feels remote and isolated and may have a strong fear of intimacy. Like the individual with wide right-hand margins, he or she tends to hold back where life and love are concerned, and the space between the lines is a visual example of the psychological space this mate demands between him or herself and the rest of the world. Closeness and cuddling may be a problem for this individual, as may be the act of sex itself. If this is your lover, it might be wise to discuss your various needs for closeness. If you feel that you are not receiving the intimacy—emotional or sexual—that you need, then you should also ask yourself what limitation of your own is attracting you to this person. Perhaps you need to develop feelings of self-worth so that you can attract a more congenial mate into your life.

Extremely narrow spaces between lines and a cramped look to the page indicate someone who may be practical in the extreme—he or she doesn't want to splurge on an extra sheet of paper! This person may be nonaesthetically oriented, preferring to concentrate on other things than the appearance or comfort value in any situation. This could mean that such a mate has a miserly approach to life and love. Why go to the movies and spend twelve dollars on tickets when you can rent an older flick and view it on the VCR at home? Or he or she may prefer to eat takeout rather than dine at even a moderately priced restaurant. If you yourself are frugal and practical, then this attitude may be perfectly acceptable, but in the extreme it can be very annoying. After all, who wants to date someone for whom romance is never a priority? If there are always practical considerations—like work, or the laundry—preventing you from seeing each other or making love, then your love affair will have very little romance indeed. If you are willing to settle for such sparse accommodations, perhaps you don't feel deserving enough of the real thing and should work to enhance your self-esteem so that you can find a mate who views you as worth impressing. Another good solution would be to discuss your needs with your lover and try to find a compromise you can both live with.

Regularity is another spatial consideration. As mentioned before, evenly spaced writing is an essential component of an emotionally balanced personality. If the spaces vary enormously from narrow to wide and everywhere in between, then the writer just isn't expressing a coherent emotional base, and you should be careful in developing a relationship because you may never know quite where you stand. In fact, large discrepancies in spacing indicate that the writer is never quite sure where he or she stands and what he or she really wants and needs, so how can you be sure of your own relative position with such a mate? Remember, though, that such a case is an extreme. Many writing samples will show some degree of irregularity—combine this with other indicators for a more well-rounded analysis.

Next check the spaces between words and letters. The relative spacing between words indicates the need for closeness to or distance from others. It is important to bear in mind that we said relative here, because the size of each person's writing is different and thus the spaces between words will have to be judged based on the overall size of the handwriting. The well-adjusted writer will have words spaced reasonably far apart, that is, far enough to separate each word and make it legible and not so far that they look isolated. Normally spaced words are an indication of a competent personality, one who is socially adept and well equipped to handle situations. Such a person is well mannered and aware of the need to approach others with tact and good taste. Obviously this mate would be a social asset to you and would know how to react in group situations. You could rely on him or her to behave appropriately anywhere while still expressing his or her basic individuality without compunction.

The individual who puts extra space between each word probably feels emotionally isolated. He or she rebels at closeness, prefers solitude to group interaction, and may feel ill-equipped to handle society's rules. If this person is a true nonconformist, you may find him or her exciting, eccentric, and very likable, but none of us can function in a vacuum, and this mate might prefer to do so. Whether he or she is choosing extreme individuality as a personal statement or simply cannot function within society, it's possible you will be held at arm's distance. He or she may date you and then disappear for weeks at a time, calling up for infrequent rendezvous—always at his or her own convenience. Perhaps this tactic is simply a way to maintain personal freedom and avoid building a relationship. But it can certainly be unpleasant for the partner who has to sit alone evenings waiting for the phone to ring!

It might be logical to assume that someone who puts extremely narrow spaces between words is capable of true intimacy, and this is true to a certain extent. This individual is a closeness junkie. He or she demands intimacy, interaction, and interdependence twenty-four hours a day. This lover can be very jealous and may spend hours quizzing you on your whereabouts if you do manage to leave his or her side. If you crave attention and need a lot of closeness yourself, you'll enjoy the lavish attention that such a lover can provide. But a more independent individual will realize that togetherness is not a synonym for smothering and will feel overwhelmed by such a mate. But if you love this person anyway, take heart. It is possible that with emotional growth on his or her part and lots of patience from you, in time this person might loosen his or her grip enough to make the relationship more comfortable.

The next overall consideration is slant. First examine the basic slant of the page as a whole. If the writing is going uphill in a pronounced direction, then the individual is an extreme optimist. In fact, he or she may never know when to quit because of this terminally positive outlook. For the most part, however, optimism is a positive quality. Most of us agree that a positive attitude can sometimes be all that's necessary for success in any endeavor. In addition, positive people are usually happy and cheerful, and nearly everyone prefers the company of such a mate. Only in a very extreme case, when the optimism is so pronounced that it acts as a hindrance to reality recognition, is it bad.

Writing that slants downhill is the sign of a pessimist, or of someone who is disappointed over a recent occurrence. It could also be an indication of the writer's opinion on the specific matter about which he is writing. Take all these possibilities into account before you label someone a true pessimist.

Look further to consider the slant of the letters them-

This is an exciting time in my life—a new job, a new home, and lots of exciting people to meet.

Normal Right Slant

selves. In most cases, the right-handed writer will slant his or her letters to the right, and the left-handed writer will slant letters to the left. For a right-handed writer, a slight right slant is a good sign, indicating that he or she is sociable and extroverted. This mate is pleasant company, enjoys going out in groups, and can hold his or her own in any conversation. If you are reasonably extroverted, you will be comfortable with such a partner because he or she has a style similar to your own. If you are a bit shy, this partner can be just what you need because he or she could compensate for your less outgoing nature.

An extreme right slant is an indication of the emotionally dependent individual. Such a person requires company all the time, and if you begin dating, expect lots of phone calls, pleas for attention, and a great amount of time spent together. This person hasn't yet developed a strong, independent personality, and like a child clinging to its mother, he or she will cling to you. If you are strong and caring, you might enjoy being a caretaker and provider of the emotional stimulation your partner needs, but eventually you might begin to feel smothered and trapped. The most fulfilling relationships are formed between people with strong, independent

When summer finally arrived the city was filled with tourists, while for the most part the natives were gone to the country or the coast.

Extreme Right Slant

personalities. Then again, a lot of love, caring, and patience could bring this mate out of his or her shell.

Letters slanting to the left indicate an extremely introverted person. Whether this individual is shy or simply aloof, he or she does not reach out to others. Such a mate may be hard to get to know and may even repel your requests for a date. If you are waiting and hoping that such a person will make the first move and ask you out, then you may have to wait for a long time. The best tactic is to get to know him or her casually by taking your time and sharing many short conversations. Perhaps this is a temporary withdrawal caused by a recent bout with heartbreak—maybe you are the lover who can help heal the wounds.

The slants described above are appropriate personality descriptions for the right-handed. For the left-handed individual, the reverse applies—a slight left slant is a sign of a well-developed, extroverted personality, and an ex-

I hope that I will be in Denver by June, but if I'm unable to make it out by then, I'll certainly be out here this summer.

Vertical Writing

treme left slant is one of emotional overdependence. A right slant indicates shyness and introversion.

Some people do not slant their letters very much, or not at all. These individuals can be emotionally restrained. Although they are aware of their own feelings, they prefer to avoid being completely open to the rest of the world. Perhaps they work in jobs that require the use of a poker face, like a judge, or perhaps they're just sensitive and have learned to control their emotions. This is neither a positive nor negative indication, as long as the individual is willing to be intimate at the appropriate times—with you if you're his or her mate!

Now let's take a look at the letters themselves. In most handwriting, the shape of the letters varies from extremely round to extremely narrow and angular, representing a continuum from emotional and sensual to controlled and spartan. Round letters indicate an individual who loves luxury, who is emotionally free and open, romantic and sensual. This mate is extremely popular and can be a lot of fun, especially in bed, because he or she lives according to the pleasure principle.

In the case of extremely round letters, the writer may be so lavish and luxury loving that he or she is incapable of the discipline necessary to earn a living. A rounded, but not obese-looking style of writing is the happy medium. This individual is sensual and appreciates pleasure, and he or she is open and emotionally available, yet is not such a prisoner to the good life that he or she refuses to go out and earn it. Such a partner is everyone's favorite, because he or she is well adjusted and a complete individual—sort of an eighties man or woman who expresses his or herself on every level.

Extremely narrow or angular letters indicate someone with a parsimonious nature. He or she is always in control, and that could mean that this mate will try to control you through emotional withdrawal or through sex. This mate refuses to go with the flow, because doing so makes him or her feel insecure. Being in charge is essential. If you are weak or disorganized and are looking for someone to take charge of your life, then this could be your ideal mate. But you still should be determined to develop your own individuality rather than seek a mate to whom you can be a subset. In the most extreme cases, this independent writer will be completely unavailable for your most intimate needs, be they emotional or physical.

Slightly angular forms can indicate the dynamic personality of a driven achiever, but one who is not completely out of touch with personal and sexual needs. If you are practical and disciplined yourself, a mate with slightly angular forms—like your own—can be an asset. Both of you will concentrate on your climb to the top of the ladder of success, and each will support the other in a need to sacrifice and strive for achievement. Like-

Every night that pathetic TV weatherman promises that the heat will let up, but every day more and more people are being broiled alive in Brooklyn.

School Type

wise, if you are a true libertine with obese letters, then perhaps you need someone practical like this who will earn the money you need to have in order to live your lavish life-style. Remember, however, that a partner with extremely angular letters will never allow you to spend his or her cash in the manner to which you'd like to become accustomed.

Check now to see how each letter is connected to every other letter. There are several different types of connecting strokes, all of which provide additional information. The *schooltype* connector features a smooth series of loops, before and after each letter, like on the lettering charts that elementary school teachers use as decoration in their classrooms. The schooltype connector, and variations on it, are very common because most Americans were taught to write this way. This type of connector is neat and regular, indicating a personality that relies on conventional teachings and society. Such a mate wants to be a good citizen and will work hard to fulfill his or her conventional role within a relationship.

The *garland* type of connector is smooth and curvy,

A day so perfect I dare not let out my breath—cloudless, dry, the sky unearthly blue, the air so clear and the sand so dazzling I know that when I shield my eyes from the glare and look across the sleeping water I will see a certain flutter at the window of the house that is miles away.

Garland Type

like the schooltype, but it flows more readily and has a more sensuous appearance. It indicates a personality that is loving, flexible, pleasure oriented, and romantic. This mate thrives on comfort and pleasure, and he or she will spend extra time and money on you and your pleasure—after all, you only live once!

The *arcade* connector features tight formations that resemble the garland type with a bit of compression. This indicates personalities that have been taught emotional control, like artistic types who were always being told to behave by their parents. Such a mate may have many dimensions to his or her personality as well as a number of hidden talents or skills. He or she may wax and wane as far as you're concerned, following the mood of the moment. Life with such a mate will never be dull!

The *angle* connector looks like its name—angular. The strokes seem dynamic and powerful as they etch their way between the letters, and you can imagine that such a writer is domineering, energetic, or filled with conflict. This person always seeks to establish control,

Pack my box with five dozen liquor jugs, to be specific make it amaretto - I love it!

Arcade Type

sometimes because he or she feels that his or her own control of any situation is slipping. This mate can be bossy and driven, and while that can be a macho turn-on in bed sometimes, it may not be comfortable or desirable in the long term.

The final connector is the *thread* type, which looks like a squiggle, moving easily from letter to letter, almost flowing together like a line. Often these writers have hard-to-read writing, for it is so connected and poorly formed that each letter seems indistinct and ready to merge with the others. These individuals are diplomatic to the extent that one is never sure on which side of any issue they stand. While this can be useful in medi-

Sorry I haven't written in so long. Things here in New York have been pretty busy. For instance, last night I did my laundry and watched TV. Isn't that great?

Angular Type

[illegible]

Thread Type

ation, it can be extremely frustrating in personal situations. But, because they are so intelligent, these people can be made to compromise—if you win them over with a sound argument.

Look at the size and shape of the letters themselves. If they are fairly wide, that indicates emotional openness. Extremely wide letters imply great emotional need, like a child who is looking for a parent to assume responsibility for him or her. The narrower the letter, the more restrained and inhibited the writer. Obviously a middle ground is the best choice, representing a partner who is willing to deal with emotional issues, who reaches out to others yet maintains his or her independence, and who is open yet in control of him or herself. Basically, that describes a well-rounded person.

The next step is to divide the lines into zones. Imagine that the sample you are looking at is written on lined paper. The line on which the letters stand is called the base line. The base line represents the division between

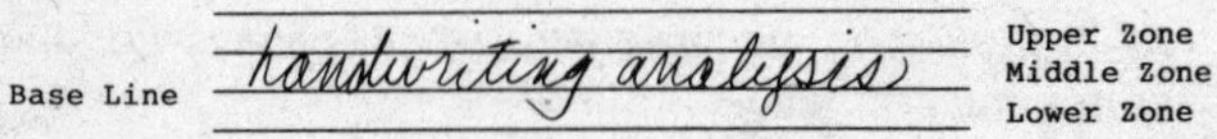

Base Line — *handwriting analysis* — Upper Zone / Middle Zone / Lower Zone

the conscious and the unconscious. Letters like a lowercase *m, s,* and *c* rest entirely on the base line. Then we divide each line of text into three zones: the middle, the upper, and the lower. The middle zone—or the area filled by the lowercase letters with no stem or tail—describes the ego. This is an indication of the individual's practicality and his or her feelings about the material world. Someone with a well-developed middle zone will have a strong ego, a good sense of material issues, and a positive expectation of prosperity. Such a partner could be a good provider, a strongly practical person who will always be able to survive in the world. A badly developed or neglected middle zone indicates a lack of these qualities or some problems with the ego and with the real world. Obviously such a partner will have a hard time with the practical aspects of a relationship, such as being able to pay the rent.

Above the middle zone is the upper zone. Letters like lowercase *l, k,* and *h* rest on the base line and extend into the upper zone. The upper zone is an indication of the individual's approach to goals, ambitions, and ideals. It also describes his or her relative intellectual orientation and spirituality. A well-emphasized upper zone is a sign of someone who has far-reaching ideals, a sense of him or herself as part of a much larger whole, and an intellectual willingness to explore the universe and his or her part in it. Such a mate will be interesting and thought provoking, because he or she is always working overtime intellectually.

This person reaches for meanings to life beyond the mundane or obvious and can always achieve more than someone whose upper zone is neglected. We can all achieve as much as we believe we can, and this lover reaches for the stars. Someone with a neglected upper zone may be so involved with practical issues, their career, for example, that he or she neglects higher truths, and sometimes personal relationships. That is not the path to happiness or success.

Below the middle zone is the lower zone. Letters like lowercase *g*, *y*, and *p* rest on the base line and extend into the lower zone, which is an indication of the unconscious, the instinct, and the individual's approach to sex and feelings about his or her body. The person with a well-developed lower zone is creative, sensitive, and possibly in tune with his or her unconscious needs. A good lower zone can indicate a high level of contentment and unselfconscious self-expression.

One way to determine the relative development of the lower zone is to see how far the letters extend into it. If they extend reasonably far, then that is a person who is sexy and interested in sex. Further information about a person's approach to sex depends on a variety of factors. Examine the loops formed below the base line. Nice curving loops indicate a strong sexual need. If the loops are rounded and close at the base line, then the individual is well adjusted and allows his or her unconscious needs to filter up through the consciousness where they can be expressed. Such a partner is sensual and sexual and will work hard to please both you and him or herself. He or she feels that sex is important and

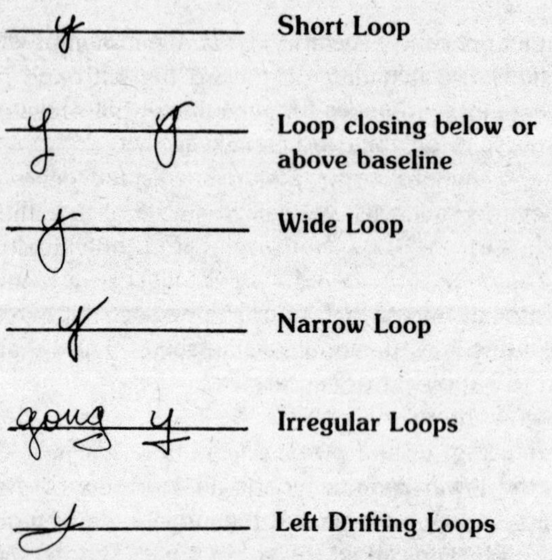

worth doing well. It is also natural and normal, and very little inhibition or embarrassment is indicated.

Other types of loops can indicate a variety of less positive approaches to sex. Loops that are short or letters that barely descend below the base line and have no loops at all indicate a disinterest in sex. Perhaps this person is too preoccupied with intellectual pursuits or too businesslike to deal with personal values and physical intimacy. Loops that close above or below the base line indicate some sexual problems, perhaps shyness, a poor body image, or an inability to let go and release enough to have an orgasm. Extremely wide loops indicate a nature that is sensual and fantasy-oriented, but one that does not manage to have satisfying sex in real life. Extremely narrow loops indicate shyness or extreme inhibition. Loops that have unusual closings or erratic shapes may indicate a certain unpredictability about sex or the need for sexual experimentation. And finally, loops that drift off toward the left-hand margin indicate immaturity and a personality that seeks nurturing through sexual involvement.

As mentioned before, regularity is the ticket. Well-developed formations in all three zones are the ideal because they indicate a well-rounded individual who is able to deal with life in an open, aggressive, confident, emotionally available way. Such people achieve success both in their careers and in relationships. And that is the kind of partner you want to find!

Let's look at an actual handwriting sample to determine the writer's personality. This is part of the note Jenna wrote to one of her prospective dates when she answered the personals.

The overall first impression of her handwriting confirms what her date told her: It is neat, precise, and pretty. Her clear, regular lettering indicates a healthy, well-developed personality. She has relatively large left-hand margins, indicating a good sense of proportion and a personality that recognizes the necessity for the social graces. Her narrow right-hand margins signal an aggressive, outgoing nature. The letters are round and reasonably curved, but not excessively so, indicating a love of pleasure but the discipline to work hard to achieve success. There is a reasonable, but not overly large or small space between words, indicating a need to relate to others but not an overwhelming obsession for smothering relationships. Likewise each line is well placed so that it can be read as a separate piece of text, yet there is no excess space. Jenna is artistic and sensitive, able to communicate and relate to others and still

I am interested in finding a soul mate, a man who will be my true love, with whom I can build a warm and wonderful life.

I like exciting, aggressive men, probably because I'm a strong woman who refuses to apologize or play games. Being my own boss is exciting, and to tell the truth, I never dreamed I'd be this successful. If you think we might be a good match, give me a call. My number is keep in touch with her own personality and sense of aesthetics. There is a great deal of energy and vitality to her hand, and a fair degree of pressure shows through to the other side of the page. This is a strong, capable, modern woman.

Her writing slants upward, indicating an optimistic nature, but one that is not blind to reality. Her letters show combined rounded and angular forms, indicating sensuousness as well as personal dynamism. Similarly, her connectors combine the garland form with occasional angle connectors, indicating an aggressive personality, but one that is emotionally open and willing to relate with others on emotional and sexual terms.

Finally, as we check her base line and zone distribution, we see relatively well-developed zones in all three areas. The middle zone shows a solid ego and practical nature; the upper zone describes a strong intellect and a spiritual, goal-oriented personality; the lower zone, with its pronounced loops that cross at the base line, shows that Jenna is more than willing to allow her sexual urges to be expressed completely and without inhibition. The fact that her writing practically jumps off the page confirms this love of sex and freedom of personal expression. When Jenna says she is an open, aggressive, modern woman who wants a soul mate with whom she can communicate at all levels, she really means it!

If you go point-by-point through a writing sample, you will learn quite a bit about the writer. Remember that each person combines several of the qualities indicated, so don't go too far overboard in your assessment. It is unlikely that you will confront a true deviant, someone who is completely unavailable emotionally, a passionate lush, or any other extreme type. Bear in mind that weaknesses or negative indications are often balanced by other factors. We are all mixed types, and it is important to remember that when doing any personality analysis, and to be careful to observe the subtle nuances before you come to conclusions, particularly if you are going to reveal what you have discovered to the subject. Be discreet and be wise!

Handwriting analysis can teach you a tremendous amount about the people in your life—and new acquaintances. Always remember to use your best instincts and a loving spirit in conjunction with your analytical skills, and you will always come out on top.

CHAPTER III

the Runes

THE SYMBOLS OF THE RUNES REPRESENT various letters of Germanic alphabets, with each letter having a meaning about a various aspect of life. The rune stones were used to interpret the mysteries of life by the very early Germanic peoples, including the Vikings. They were used not just as predictive tools, but as powerful talismans, to be carved on swords, shields, and larger stones.

One early story of the power of the runes sounds a lot like the fable of Sleeping Beauty. The high priestess Sigfried lay sleeping at the top of a sacred mountain, protected from invasion—and escape—by a giant ring of flames that was all but impenetrable. Her true love, Sigurdhr, challenges both the mountain and the flames with the help of a horse with magical powers. Sigurdhr wakes Sigfried, and they exchange vows of love. Then she imparts to him essential wisdom based on runic messages. This act binds them forever into one unit, one soul, one force for earthly triumph. It is through their union that both achieve a new level of evolution—both ascending to a higher plane of self-expression, and each joining the other at the highest soul level possible.

The ancient vision described by the runes can seem rather complex to the modern student and sometimes even a bit passé. The specific messages of the runic stones often have to do with crops, horses, winter and waiting, summer and harvest. Those of us who don't live on farms have to make a quantum leap of imagination to translate this wisdom into modern applications. This is done for you here. Each description is geared toward the modern reader, yet each contains the very essence of the rune's message.

The issues described by the runes are actually not that complex. They say that we must all develop our individuality to its maximum potential, and then we can find the soul mate who will complete our life's journey. They say that it is essential to nourish and receive sustenance from both the family and society. Goals are important in the runic system, as is the perseverance necessary to achieve success through hard work. Prosperity and joy are the natural conditions of life—if we are on the right path. In a certain sense, the runic message almost sounds like the Boy Scout Credo—which is, after all, a very positive point of view.

The real point is that the runes have tremendous power to educate us all about our approaches to life, love, money, and success, and even in the modern world we can benefit from their wisdom. As you begin asking questions and turn to the rune interpretation section, you will discover something amazing—the messages speak right to your very heart, and they explore with astounding accuracy the very question that puzzles you. They can guide you out of a problem, or lead you in a better direction. The runes can show you what you're doing to attract misfortune and how to release this negativity. Or they can encourage you to keep on plugging away. It all depends on you!

Your first step in doing rune readings is to get a set of runes. They are available in new age and other book stores throughout the country, or you may want to make your own runes, which was the tradition among rune-masters. They carved their runes out of the wood from sacred trees, and you could do that, but even if you could locate the sacred trees, it would be quite time consuming. An easy first set of runes can be made from thin cardboard. Simply cut the cardboard into twenty-five squares and draw the appropriate symbol on each. Be sure to follow the designs precisely, as some are quite similar. Leave the last one blank. You can store your runes in a plastic bag. If you want a more elaborate set, river rocks, like those popular among florists, or small pebbles are excellent. You can easily paint the symbols on the rocks. Once again, a plastic bag is good for storage. (Runes are traditionally kept in a suede pouch.)

Once you have bought or made your runes, you'll be ready to begin doing readings. Let's go through a number of possible methods now. Then you can choose the method that most appeals to you. Follow that technique, turning to the rune interpretation section to learn the meanings of the runes you have selected.

The first technique is the most obvious. Simply voice your question, close your eyes, concentrate on the question, and reach into your rune pouch and withdraw one rune. Then check its meaning.

Elizabeth wanted to do the first reading. She knows that she is ready for a romance with a real soul mate, and two different psychics have predicted such a love affair coming soon. She still wants confirmation, however, for she has been seeking this lover for a long time. Elizabeth's question is, "What will happen in my love life in the next six weeks?" She draws number 24, *Sowelu*, the rune representing God and the perfect integration of the spirit. Sowelu represents achieving one's own perfection—the ultimate completion possible for a soul on earth. This is a wonderful sign for Elizabeth, for it indicates that she is now operating at a very high energy level and is ready not just to meet a lover, but to connect with a true soul mate who is also highly evolved and who will complete her very existence.

Sharon is concerned about Mark, a man whom she loves but who is involved with someone else, albeit unhappily. Sharon thinks about Mark all the time. Sometimes she feels that he will snap to his senses and will free himself from his current entanglement so that they can be together, since she's sure they truly belong together. At other times, Sharon acknowledges that her love life hasn't been very happy for many years, and since a long-ago heartbreak, she has been very guarded about falling in love because she fears another broken heart. Perhaps her obsession for Mark is simply another excuse to keep her out of the meat market and away from potential lovers, and maybe she should release it. Her question is "What will happen between Mark and me in the future?"

Sharon chooses number 5, *Uruz*, the rune representing inevitable transformation. The message of this rune is positive but unclear. Uruz informs Sharon that she is now in the process of releasing the blocks that have held her back and that true happiness and pure love are at hand. Since this rune describes releasing elements from the past, Sharon could infer that she is being asked to let go of her obsession for Mark—and that is probably good advice. But since she asked about her and Mark, it is also possible to conclude that the things that have separated them are being released and that they will live happily ever after. In any case, Sharon is promised happiness—once she releases her inner blocks to attaining it. In a situation such as this when conflicting messages occur, it is because the future isn't yet formed. Only the part about Sharon's happiness is available now. The details of that happiness can go either way—with Mark or with someone else, and that is the attitude that Sharon should take.

Barbara learns from Sharon's answer and decides to ask a more specific question: "What must I do to attract a lover?" She is ready, willing, and able, and will follow the advice of the runes without bringing to bear any of her old emotional baggage. She draws number 22, *Dagaz*, the rune representing metaphysical knowledge and mind-expanding points of view. Dagaz is asking Barbara to develop her psychic potential in her search for true love. In other words, Barbara should use meditation and creative visualization to attract her perfect soul mate. She should focus on the man of her dreams, not as a specific vision, but as a blank ideal to which the universe can fill in the details in Barbara's own best interest. If she asks for her true love, the one perfect man for her will be forthcoming.

* * *

A more complicated reading stems from a technique called runic cross. In it, six runes are chosen and are laid out in a cross shape. It is much easier visually and contextually to lay the stones in a circle or a simple line, however, and none of the power of the reading will be lost if you do this instead. You can approach this technique in two ways. First voice the question. Then either choose six stones randomly and interpret them according to the six definitions that follow; or first voice the question, then voice the first definition, choose a stone to embody it, voice the second definition, choose a stone, and so on. Do whatever feels most comfortable to you.

These are the six definitions:

1) your past
2) who you are now—your current issues
3) developing circumstances
4) the foundation for the question (past circumstances)
5) challenges for you to overcome
6) the results

Janet asked simply for some insights about her love life. In position one, her past, Janet chose number 7, *Nauthiz*, the rune that demands that we all build our own lives with care. Nauthiz warns Janet that the romantic disappointments of her past have influenced her present by building up fears of relationships that she must be sure to release.

In position two, who she is now, Janet chose number 14, *Kano*, a rune of self-expression and acceptance. Janet has come a long way toward self-understanding and is now ready to express the complete essence of her being. She is in touch with her emotional and sexual needs—which she once was not—and she is willing to let them be the essential part of her life that they should be. This is a good sign that she is making the kind of progress she wishes to make, for only as a complete human being can any of us merge with a soul mate.

In position three, the developing circumstances, Janet chose number 13, *Jera*, the rune of fruition. Jera promises success when all the appropriate steps toward that success are taken. In other words, Janet had problems that she is working patiently to release. She's achieved self-knowledge and the determination to meet her essential needs, and here we see she is likely to get what she wants.

In position four, the foundation for wanting a happy love life, Janet chose number 10, *Algiz reversed* (upside down). This rune warns of a danger of the spirit. Janet is still afraid to believe that her true love will indeed come along, and thus she is tempted to compromise and take just any lover, because after all, she is lonely. Since this is the foundation, it is an indication of Janet's modus operandi in the past. She has compromised on love before, so no wonder she hasn't found happiness! Algiz is cautioning her not to do this any longer, but to hold out for true love.

In position five, Janet's challenge, she chose number 5, *Uruz reversed*, indicating a need to explore her own psyche further. Janet concentrates on others too much and herself too little. Uruz is challenging her to work harder to know her own needs—her past and present—in other words, to examine her life and see how her past decisions have created her present.

In position six, the results or Janet's future, she chose

20, *Raido*, representing balance and order. There are structures that support us all, and such structures will soon be part of Janet's life, because she is ready to expand her limits to include more of the universe. In other words, Janet has been alone, but soon will have more support in her life. That could mean that Janet's personal growth will lead to a committed relationship, such as a marriage, and marriage is one of the foundations of society. We can see that Janet received a complicated message about her own life and her life patterns. She has been demanding too little of the universe, because she was not ready to develop herself to the extent that she would be able to interact with it on many levels. Now she is working to become a more complete human being, and with that completion will come greater happiness, more support from the universe, and true love.

Another similar reading technique has the following definitions:

1) the current situation
2) your hopes and wishes
3) your hidden fears or obstacles
4) the right path for you to pursue
5) the best results you can hope for

Robert is involved in a difficult relationship, yet he doesn't seem to be able to leave his lover. He asked for insight into his situation. In position one, the current situation, he chose number 21, *Thurisaz*, representing the forces of the universe that intervene when we refuse to make our own choices. Robert is being challenged to take a stand and do something about his situation, or else he will experience this crisis from without—through his girlfriend's actions or other unwelcome circumstances. Thurisaz is offering him encouragement, for Robert has the ability to make the right choice.

In position two, his hopes and wishes, Robert chose number 12, *Wunjo*, representing joy. He is romantic and he believes in happily-ever-after endings—and so do the runes. But he has to be on the right path, in the right stream of energy for Wunjo to pay off. That is an essential fact about the universe and the joy it grants. And just as that is an important truth, so is its opposite—if Robert lacks joy, then he is on the wrong path.

In position three, his fears and obstacles, Robert chose number 11, *Fehu reversed*, indicating a fear of happiness and a tendency to compromise. Robert needs the faith to reach for his true heart's desire, not for tacky substitutes. In position four, Robert's right path, he chose number 17, *Ehwaz*, representing support systems. Robert should reach out to the people he trusts and seek support in his quest for a better life. That could include a visit to a therapist or counselor.

In the last position, the best possible results, Robert drew number 15, *Teiwaz reversed*, indicating a need to develop a better personal value system. When Robert gets better in touch with his own needs, the negativity of his current relationship will no longer be a magnet for him, and he will be able to release it. The runes here are telling Robert that his unhappy love affair is the result of an unhealthy approach to life, one that he is clinging to out of fear. He needs to develop better patterns for himself, and then a better relationship can come into his life.

* * *

A final method of reading the runes is simply to mix up the runes in the bag and dump them all out onto the floor, whether you voice a specific question or not. Then read the meanings of those that fall face up and return to the bag those that reveal only their backs. Upside-down runes can be read, since their symbols are visible. If too many fall right side up, start over.

Alison got the following six runes: numbers 1, 2, 4, 9, 18, and 5. Number 1, *Mannaz*, asks Alison to keep working to develop her individuality. Number 2, *Gebo*, suggests that she will be receiving some well-earned rewards, such as more money or a true love. Number 4, *Othila*, once again suggests new benefits coming, whether through family solidarity, an inheritance, or just loving ties. So far, it looks as though Alison's life is improving, because she was concerned about both money and love. Perhaps they will be combined in the form of a lover to whom she can make a commitment and later marry, combining emotional and material resources.

Number 9, *Inguz*, predicts fulfillment and perhaps a whole new life, just as we had guessed. Number 18, *Laguz*, represents nurturing through emotional development. It suggests that there will be a deeply fulfilling emotional tie that will allow Alison to receive great joy. Number 5, *Uruz*, predicts that Alison will become a completely new person, able to receive true love and happiness. What a reading! It would seem that Alison is on the threshold of a whole new life, promising her emotional fulfillment, self-expression, money, and true love. You can't beat that!

As you can see, rune readings provide the deepest of information, and they are unfailingly honest. If you're unwilling to face a part of yourself, the runes are not a good choice for you, for they will hone in on this weakness immediately and caution you to release it and to see yourself and your life with the honesty that is essential for progress. There is no set destiny awaiting you, however, and the runes are very clear about that fact. You are creating your own life, day by day, and every moment you experience is a result of something you have set into motion in the past. You, and only you, have the power to change your life from bad to good. The runes show you how.

THE RUNES INTERPRETED

1. Mannaz represents human individuality as tied into the universe at large. You have developed yourself to a certain extent, but there is more work to be done. Yes, you have made great progress, but don't let the pride in your own accomplishments stop you from growing farther. You are still in a formative stage. Greater knowledge of your own task and the purpose that guides you is at hand. Relax and let yourself receive inspiration, whether from your family, a mentor, or simply the forces of the universe. When you are completely centered in yourself and in the present that governs your every moment, you will be able to move ahead. For now, go slowly.

Mannaz reversed is an indication that you are placing stumbling blocks in your own path. We are each the only source of our disappointments. Examine what surrounds you and consider what you have done to attract these conditions to yourself. Then release them. Have faith in the universe and in your own ability to choose well.

2. Gebo represents justified rewards. You have developed your individuality and now you are ready to be part of a greater whole. That could mean that you are about to embark on a new and more fulfilling relationship with a lover, or that someone who will share your life in another area will come along, such as a business partner or a new friend. You are ready to receive rewards, and whether you get a true love, a gift, or a bonus, you deserve it and will know how to handle it.

3. Ansuz represents knowledge being transferred from a powerful force to one receptive to that power. You are about to graduate to a new level of personal development. You are ready to pay more attention to the events that surround you and thereby receive greater self-knowledge and more insight into the ways of the world. With this information you can go on to have a more fulfilling life. You may be ready to make more and greater commitments to develop yourself. You can access greater psychic power or greater earthly power. Perhaps you will help another to live, as in a woman who decides to become pregnant. In any case, what you reach toward is better than whatever you are leaving behind. Life is always an upward spiral, and it's time for you to grow.

Ansuz reversed indicates that you have been trapped

in confusion for some time, and therefore you feel despair, but you have the power to release the traps that are making you miserable. Don't feel that your life has no meaning just because you can't see the horizon you face. Reach for clarity and greater understanding. Do not accept confusion any longer, because once you repudiate it, you will release whatever it is that binds it to you.

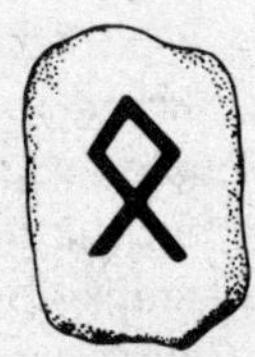

4. Othila represents the strength of the family, the forces of society, and the security resulting from belonging to a whole larger than one's self. You are reaffirming your ties to the group. Whether that means that you are growing closer to a family member or are part of a neighborhood, club, or organization that makes you feel nourished, you are gaining strength from those around you. You may even receive some benefits as a result of your group ties. This could be actual money, as in an inheritance, a new level of knowledge or awareness as a result of a mentor's guidance, or simply the opportunity to take advantage of group privileges, like a special travel rate for groups only. The point is that you are enhancing your own position by being a part of a larger whole. That does not mean, of course, that your individuality is unimportant. On the contrary, individuality is always an essential first step in every area of life. Once you are a true individual, you can both contribute to and receive from the group.

Othila reversed indicates that you are about to embark on a radical new path, but that it will be right for you. Tradition is useful only as long as it nourishes. Once the meaning is gone, you are free to seek new forms of sustenance. Open yourself up to these new possibilities. If you feel alienated for a time, allow that to be, for at the brink of every new life path is some degree of doubt and insecurity. You will be making new connections that will be more meaningful than previous ones if you allow this change to take place.

5. Uruz represents the inevitable growth that occurs through life. Now it is up to you to allow a regeneration of your psyche. Not only is a new stage of your life about to begin, you will be a new, almost completely different person. Don't worry about these changes, because they are always for the best. Like a snake shedding an old skin, you will reveal a shiny new self to the world. Right now you may be frightened, because though you have released elements from your past that once had almost overwhelming holds on you, it may be too early yet to see where the future will lead you. You are in the dark, but the moment of light is at hand. You will be stronger, more confident, and far more capable of independence and happiness in the future. Trust that the future will be a vast improvement on the past. The sources of true happiness or pure love that formerly eluded you may now be within your grasp.

Uruz reversed indicates that you have not been paying enough attention to yourself. Take the time now to examine your own life and your own soul. Learn about who you truly are and don't be afraid to face yourself and your life in the mirror. Awareness and conscious determination are the two essential tools of every life. This is your chance to have them.

6. Perth represents the mysterious forces of the universe that seem to hold us in the palm of their hand. However, the truth is that these forces are not in charge of you; they are merely giving you a push toward the destiny that you have chosen all along. You have set out to meet certain challenges in this lifetime as a means of personal and spiritual growth. Be assured that the universe is helping you in your quest. If it feels that you are being led in a new direction, it is your responsibility to seek understanding—first of where you have been, secondly of who you are, and finally that where you are headed is right. The choice is always yours.

Perth reversed indicates challenges in your path. It is tempting to try to avoid the stress of going where you have not yet mastered the way. Avoid this negative approach to life. Yes, you are experiencing difficulties, but they are the lessons you need to learn now in order to create a better future. The present will always turn into the future. With a graceful approach the journey will be less difficult.

7. Nauthiz represents the need to be thorough, to acknowledge that we are the creators—whether directly or indirectly—of all we experience and that hard work and patience are essential to success. You may feel that things are not going well for you in a certain area of your life. You feel that perhaps it is your destiny to fail in this area. You're wrong. You need to reach inside yourself and uncover the fears and limitations you have constructed that hold you back. Once

you are completely in touch with what is wrong, you can work to release it. Don't assume that this will happen overnight, however. Keep uncovering your own secrets and releasing your own blocks. Gradually you will feel yourself grow lighter as they fade away. Eventually they will no longer be issues, and you will be free to create your own success.

Nauthiz reversed indicates that you are fighting the process of self-discovery. You'd rather rail at the universe than seek answers inside yourself. Obviously, this won't work. First you must acknowledge that you are the source of all your own problems. Once you do that, a great power will be yours: the power to change yourself and thus to change your world. You, and only you, can accomplish this task. Dig in and commit yourself to doing it in the most positive way possible. Your most severe enemy is inside of you—release that inner struggle and all others will be easy.

8. Inguz represents fulfillment. Once you have cleared away the ashes of your old life or your former self, you are ready to begin again, not as one looking fearfully into the darkness and wondering what will come out of it, but rather as one who has braved the darkness with trust and courage and is now facing the dawn and the light. You are now on the new and better path that was promised in previous runes. You may be ready to start a new life adventure, such as a career, a love affair, or a marriage. You have prepared and have shown yourself worthy. This is your time of reward, and in accepting your new path, you have signaled that your former life is now completed.

9. Eihwaz represents the need for progress. There may be obstacles in your path, but it is not the obstacles themselves that are causing you so much stress, but rather your burning desire to get rid of them immediately. These issues will be resolved in good time. Take your time and do exactly what you must to make things right. A hasty solution is not necessarily the best. There is no deadline in life—even death waits until a suitable completion is achieved. Your problems require this approach. Perseverance is essential. Eventually you will see your problems dissolve and you will be amazed that you ever worried about them at all.

10. Algiz represents security. You need to develop or focus on your source of inner strength, that is, the faith that the universe will always support your efforts when your heart is pure and you are doing your best. This faith will protect you, acting as a shield of light that buffers you from anything that might harm you. Once this light is on, you have the ability to make the right choices and to follow your true path.

Algiz reversed indicates that there are some unsavory influences around you and that you could be in danger. This implies a danger of the spirit; you may be tempted to turn away from your center and embrace a false hope instead. No wonder you are having problems! But you will not be destroyed by these circumstances, because the universe is still on your side. All that remains is for you to believe in yourself. That faith is what you lost in the first place!

11. Fehu represents good fortune and prosperity. You are in a lucky period, and it is as though the fates have smiled upon you, delivering money, success, or great love. This is your time of happiness and prosperity. You may be ready to make a commitment—even marriage—to your partner, to decide to have a child, or to reap great financial rewards. It falls to you only to appreciate what you have received and to use it well. Abundance is not only everyone's right, it is a privilege that we all must acknowledge. Give thanks for your good luck.

Fehu reversed indicates that you have a problem with happiness and prosperity. Things are not working out in your life; you are feeling desperate and are clinging to what you have, for you fear that you will lose it. Examine your feelings about life. Have you sold yourself in bondage to a career or a spouse you don't love simply for money, only to lose the money as well as your happiness? Ask yourself what your true heart's desire is and then make a path in your life toward that end. If you have to give up what you have now to do that, it means that these things form the prison that is keeping you from your true destiny. Release the walls of doubt and doom and let the sunshine in. You can be broke and happy if you have inner knowledge. You don't have to be broke, however; you can have prosperity and success as a natural result of having the courage to pursue whatever you truly love. Selling out always sells you short.

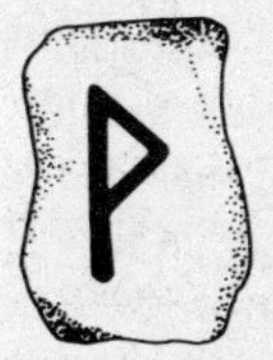

12. Wunjo represents joy. You have reached a point of true centeredness, and thus your every action radiates with light and positive energy. Because you are in the right place—emotionally, physically, and spiritually—your efforts result in rewards. You haven't happened on any great secret, nor have you gone beyond your earthly rights—this is simply the way life was always meant to be. You have fallen into the right stream of energy, as though you had stepped onto a conveyor belt and were moving effortlessly toward your chosen destination. Every area of your life is either good or improving. You can have success and happiness and a joyous relationship with a soul mate, because you are ready to accept all the good things that life has to offer.

Wunjo reversed indicates that you will achieve the success you seek but that it will take time and effort. It can be tempting to abandon a project, a love affair, or a marriage in the middle, because it sometimes seems that the desired results will never materialize. This is a test of your inner strength and personal resolve. The lessons you must learn are immutable; if you abandon the current circumstance, another, similar one will simply take its place until you develop resolve and the trust to see you through to a happy conclusion. Simply decide to have faith and keep working toward your goals.

13. Jera represents fruition after appropriate preparation. Like Wunjo, Jera promises success, not through the flow of spiritual purpose but rather as a result of the natural flow of earthly life. You have taken all the appropriate steps and have been patient, biding your time for the hoped-for result. Such a result is now at hand. You can discern when your reward will arrive simply by examining the process that you have begun. If you have planted a seed, read the package to know when a sprout will appear. An investment will come to term as indicated. A baby will be born after nine months. Each act is a series of small moments of progress leading to the next step. Enjoy the task as you go along and you will reap many more rewards, because each step toward fruition can be its own reward.

14. Kano represents the pure, uncomplicated expression and acceptance of the self. You are at a point of opening. If you were embarrassed in the past by some facet of your personality or of your passions or sexual desires, you will no longer be ill at ease with these primal urges. They are an important part of yourself that deserves expression, respect, and ultimately love. With this self-acceptance you can go on to create great things, from an artistic masterpiece to a better, deeper, more intimate relationship. You represent the greatest gift that you can share—with the universe or with a lover. By unblocking yourself, you open up to the world and you receive a chance for life and love at their fullest.

Kano reversed indicates that you are about to take a

new step. Right now you feel blocked, however, because you realize that the past is no longer valid. You may be giving up a career or a love affair because you know that you are no longer fulfilled by it. But where will you go from there? For now that important question has no answer. That doesn't mean, however, that you should return to what has served you before, because if you do, you will not be available to what is coming anew. The hardest part of progress is waiting for it to begin by opening up to new opportunities that have yet to arrive. That is your task now.

15. Teiwaz represents courage. You are strong and capable and have the courage of your convictions. At the heart of such courage is the knowledge of who you are and what your destiny will be. This is your virtue, or one that you can now try to develop. With the courage to express your inner self directly and honestly comes a simplicity that is its own reward. Those who would challenge and disagree are not attracted to you because they know that you are invincible. You can take the steps required, knowing that you are your own protector and are safe.

Teiwaz reversed indicates a need to examine your own personal power base. Are you seeking to dominate others simply out of fear that they might otherwise dominate you? The cause for such an approach is insecurity. You are not as sure of everything as you say you are. Understand that people who are secure in themselves never have to do battle over personal issues. The battle you are currently in is a test of your own beliefs, and if you work to develop a philosophy of life that will truly serve you, these conflicts will disappear.

16. Berkana represents birth. You are ready to begin something important. That could mean a marriage, a pregnancy, or a professional undertaking, but whatever it is, it will be significant. There are few true beginnings in life, since most enterprise is a result of being in the middle or at the end of something else. Here you are at square one, and that is a very potent position. It is good to acknowledge that you are at a true beginning here, and to acknowledge that you also have had a past that has been put to rest. Enjoy this new start.

Berkana reversed indicates problems. Your past is interfering with both the present and the future. Perhaps you have been hasty and thus are ill prepared for the step you are about to take. Retrace your steps like a good detective and see where you made your mistake. Be careful, be thorough, be prepared, and when you are sure you are truly ready, begin again.

17. Ehwaz represents transition achieved through interdependence. You are not alone: There are people and even machines that are essential to your progress. It's important to acknowledge this because it makes you see how much a part of society and the universe at large you are. You have certain goals now—whether to change jobs, achieve new success, relocate, establish a family. These are lofty aims and may be intimidating at first, but the support and aid

you need to help you on your journey will always be there.

Ehwaz reversed indicates a need to examine the choices you are making. Don't deceive yourself into thinking that your motives are other than they are. That is a sure way toward failure. Don't decide that the only route for yourself is escape, because escape is always temporary as well as a waste of precious time. Understand what it is that you truly need, what you really want, and then decide where you should be. A change in course is probably indicated, and the sooner you stop avoiding responsibility for your life, the sooner your life will become what you would like it to be.

18. Laguz represents all the various reservoirs of energy, including the life-giving seas, the amniotic fluids, the emotions, and the psyche and its intuitive power. You are in touch with—or need to explore—your own emotional depths. Many of the forces of life are unconscious; that is the way of nature. But the enlightened spirit brings these hidden sources out of the darkness and up into consciousness so that there can be greater understanding of ourselves and of the forces that compel us. Be willing to receive and make sense of the inspiration that guides you. Receptivity to your inner self is all it takes to receive great wisdom and enlightenment. With the understanding of your own soul comes the ability to have a happier, more fulfilling life. You will be able to comprehend your own nature and to express your deepest needs. Thus you will be able to succeed at whatever makes you happy. You will find the love that fuels your soul, whether through a roman-

tic tie or through nurturing another as a parent. The forces of life are mighty, and though they are mysterious, it is up to you to try to understand those that are at work within yourself.

Laguz reversed indicates that you have a fear of emotional things, which you must now work to overcome. There is nothing hidden inside yourself that is dark or gloomy. Your deepest instincts will lead to love, joy, and sustenance. Be willing to uncover the shadowy hiding places within your psyche and to make room for the blessings that belong there.

19. Hagalaz represents the realization of potential inherent in every corner of the universe. Just as a tulip bulb can be sliced in half to reveal the formed tulip inside, so does every beginning contain the code for the finished whole. You need to get in touch with your essential purpose. In this lifetime you have things to experience and lessons to learn. These are your reasons for living now, because you are on a path between what you have been in past lifetimes and what you endeavor to become in distant futures. The seed of your future lives in your present reality and is bursting forth from the soil of your past experience.

Take some time to examine your recent past and see where you seem to be heading. Are you making progress? Perhaps you are lacking a center and need reaffirmation that your direction is the right one for you. Can you look back on the past with forgiveness for mistakes and pride in accomplishments? Can you see a more worthy self in today's actions than you showed yesterday? That is your goal. As long as you are willing to move toward your progress unhaltingly, like the tulip coming to bloom, the process will not be difficult. Should you choose instead to block progress by clinging to the here and now or the past, the universe will challenge you to win. On the other hand, when you triumph over your foolish fears, it is not just the universe that will win, because ultimately it is always you who must win. You must meet your destiny as surely as a tulip must grow from its bulb. The rule to follow is face your future and put the past behind you—never the reverse.

20. Raido represents balance, order, logic, and ritual. Before you can make progress in any area, you must first understand the workings of that part of life. Thus if you want to be a carpenter, you must learn how to use a hammer and nails first. If you want to be an astrologer, you must learn about the planets and their correlations to man. Within the universe there is no chaos anywhere. Everything is formed to interrelate, to connect and to disconnect, each according to its place within the larger scheme of things. Seek your own means of self-expression, always remembering to learn your craft before you endeavor to use it. There is nothing worse than a practitioner who lacks skill.

You may feel that you have something to do, but that you are going at it alone. That is never true, not even of the most private journey of the soul. In every walk of life there is a network of support that can teach, guide, and inform you about both your progress and your growth. Take advantage of the structures that exist to support your efforts, whatever they are, and be sure that you contribute more than you withdraw.

Raido reversed indicates that you are too wrapped up in yourself, and thus you are walking a solitary path. This is the loneliest mistake any of us can make. If you are refusing love because you need the constant ego boost of new infatuations, you will wind up more unhappy than gratified, because you will always have only yourself at the core of your being, while others have much more. If you are trying to do complicated work without the benefit of previous knowledge, then your job is much harder and you will not go as far. Let yourself be a part of the stream of life, and it will support you and give you more of what you think you can achieve better on your own.

21. Thurisaz represents the power generated by essential opposing forces, like the tremendous burst of energy that is released through the splitting of the atom. You are feeling a sense of urgency similar to the throes of passionate sexual arousal—release is all you desire. This is a good sign that you have great power at your disposal. The challenge here is to use that power wisely and well. In every life there are several crises requiring action. These form major turning points in your life, and you are at such a point now. It is as though the universe is prodding you to take a step, and you may sense that the future will never be the same again. You're right. But don't fear this time or doubt your ability to choose well. Release your fear and ask for guidance from the forces that surround you. Even if you can choose only one of two potential paths, the choice can always be positive, no matter which path you

take. The point now is to receive inspiration and to act upon it.

Thurisaz reversed indicates that you are somewhere in the middle of your journey. You have made certain choices and now that you see a few obstacles in your path, you're inclined to rescind your decision in an effort to reclaim the past. Of course, this is impossible. Every challenge you face is an opportunity to better define your choices and to form your life according to your true desires. Be patient and stalwart and you will succeed.

22. Dagaz represents leaps of consciousness beyond earthly perception to a point where greater truths can be revealed. This is the rune of the metaphysician. You may have entered a new realm of thought where ideas and far-reaching concepts seem to radiate magically through your mind. Thus your perception of everything, even the most minor, most concrete part of reality, is shaded by a larger sense of truth. This is a good sign that you have evolved to a point of great wisdom and understanding.

You may have a talent or a psychic gift that could benefit yourself and those around you. Do not fear such abilities—there is nothing inside you to fear, only gifts that deserve rejoicing. A trip to metaphysical understanding is always a journey into the light, providing strength, power, understanding, and love. Take advantage of this opportunity to expand yourself and your universe.

23. Isa represents the need for focus. You are at a point where you may want to see some movement and some results. Don't be so hasty. You have not yet reached your center of absolute determination, and thus more time and sustained action is needed. The act of focusing is an essential part of life. In digging a flower garden, there are three steps: the first of initial ground-breaking; the final of planting the seeds. In the middle is the long period of digging, repeating step after step of inserting the shovel and lifting away the earth. This is where you are now, and it is easy at such a time to forget the joyful urge that compelled you to begin this task and to lose sight of the end result—the success of your garden. Focus will teach you discipline—which may well be a sore point with you already—and help you gain a wider viewpoint that encompasses all the steps of your project. When you have achieved this ability to remain in the present, while keeping sight of the future and also retaining the memory of the initial impulse, you will be ready to move on to a new stage of development, one that lets you receive more rewards through the actual process of doing, rather than just through having done.

24. Sowelu represents divinity and the ultimate aim of all evolution. You are reaching for your own divine connection, and you do that by finding and expressing your very best self. Inside of you is the purest of God's energy, and it is that energy that we are all trying to reach, to express, and to become a part of. Just as creation marked an act of separation from

the primal state that existed prior to it, evolution is the journey back to that state of oneness. Perhaps you are reaching out to others with selfless service. Maybe you have joined in love with the soul mate who completes your life path while still nourishing your individuality. These are signs that you are reaching for the divine inside of you. When you are on this path, life becomes easier. You know that the universe is supporting your efforts and that you will be cared for. To give the ego over to the service of the divine is to nourish the self and to access all of the loving support the universe can offer.

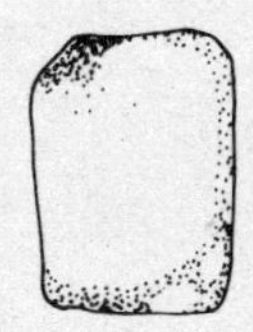

25. The Blank Rune represents purity and total trust. At the beginning of all creation, we were all characterized by blankness, that is, the lack of both experience and knowledge. At the end of this cycle of evolution, when all claims of ego have been released in favor of a oneness that represents pure spirit, pure joy, and pure love, there will be blankness again. Blankness describes the release of specific experience. Perhaps that is the state you currently seek to embody now. You may have resolved your life issues and are now seeking a more evolved path. If you are truly without ego, then you will wait for the universe to point you in the direction that will most benefit it, because you are no longer a self-demanding fulfillment but rather an impulse desiring to serve greater channels. This goal takes courage, but courage is easy and natural when you are evolved to this point. Joy is a state of fulfillment so great that no other fuel is needed.

the runic alphabet

	NAME	CATCHWORDS
1.	*Mannaz*	self-development; individuality
2.	*Gebo*	justified rewards
3.	*Ansuz*	knowledge; information
4.	*Othila*	family; closeness and support
5.	*Uruz*	inevitable growth; releasing karma
6.	*Perth*	mysterious forces
7.	*Nauthiz*	thoroughness; patience
8.	*Inguz*	fulfillment; personal triumph
9.	*Eihwaz*	progress; perseverance
10.	*Algiz*	security; faith
11.	*Fehu*	prosperity; good fortune
12.	*Wunjo*	joy
13.	*Jera*	fruition; material success
14.	*Kano*	self-expression; self-acceptance
15.	*Teiwaz*	courage
16.	*Berkana*	birth; beginnings
17.	*Ehwaz*	society; support systems
18.	*Laguz*	nurturing resevoirs
19.	*Hagalaz*	realization; personal growth

20. *Raido*	ritual; balance; order
21. *Thurisaz*	nuclear energy; transformation
22. *Dagaz*	metaphysics; awareness; mysticism
23. *Isa*	focus; discipline; sustained action
24. *Sowelu*	divinity; oneness
25. *Blank Rune*	lack of experience; blankness

CHAPTER IV

Body Language

HOW MANY TIMES WHILE YOU WERE GROWING up did a parent or teacher give you the following advice? "Stand up straight." "Shake hands firmly and decisively, not like a limp fish." "Smile when you meet someone new." Most of us look back on childhoods filled with admonishments like those above, and we know as adults how much sense they make. Though the grown-ups in our lives may not have realized it at the time, the advice they were giving so often was about positive body language, and their goal was to help us with unwritten, unspoken expressions of positive personality traits.

Body language is a series of messages sent out through gesture and movement that signify how we really feel about ourselves, our companions, and life in general. What if you were with someone new, having a pleasant conversation, both of you smiling in a friendly way. The casual exchange would imply a developing relationship. The words easily shared would indicate an intellectual compatibility. It would seem that you and your new acquaintance were off to a good start.

But, to complicate the picture, what if he or she were fidgeting uncontrollably? Twitching? Itching and scratching? Crossing and uncrossing a pair of legs that are in constant motion? You would get a far different message from your companion—he or she is nervous or ill at ease. Perhaps you would wonder if your conversation were holding up a more pressing engagement. Or maybe you would conclude that there was something wrong with you—that the other party did not really find you interesting at all. All of these messages come from body language. Even though all the other signs had been positive, the overwhelming negative body language could not be ignored.

We are all students of body language, but usually the messages we receive and send out are unconscious. By bringing some of the unconscious signals out into the light where we can examine them, we can gain great power and knowledge. First of all, we have a much clearer, more easily accessible picture of what our friends and lovers are feeling. In an obvious example like a first date or job interview, this information can be invaluable. Secondly, by learning about both positive and negative body language, we can consciously take control of our own hidden messages and exchange the less than positive ones for stronger, more definitive gestures that really get across what we wish to convey. Thus we ourselves can control not only our own behavior, but other people's perceptions of us, and that is truly a powerful and enviable position to be in. Let's look at a few scenarios in which body language plays an essential role. Then we can decide if it's favorable or unfavorable, and if so, what improvements or changes are necessary.

Sharon and Elliot are at a singles event. Sharon is standing near the dance floor, watching the dancers. When Elliot sees her, he feels an instant attraction. He walks over and begins a conversation, and as they talk, in general there is a good intellectual rapport. There are no awkward pauses, and each is comfortable communicating with the other. Then they begin to dance. Both Sharon and Elliot enjoy expressing themselves to the music. Later they return to the sidelines to continue their conversation.

But although Sharon enjoys taking to this man, she is not attracted to him at all. Why not? First of all, Elliot is small and thin, and Sharon prefers tall, athletic types. That is something that neither party can help, but Sharon is not unreasonably prejudiced against short men if they have a physical presence. But Elliot has none. He stands in a drooping way. His shoulders slump. His stomach protrudes, despite the fact that he is not at all overweight. He is a listless dancer. Sharon classifies him as a wimp. The fact that they have a good rapport means nothing, because Sharon finds Elliot physically unappealing. When he asks for her number, she makes an excuse. When she tries to go to another area of the room, Elliot doesn't take the hint, but follows her instead, making a pest of himself.

Finally Sharon is forced to be honest. She is there to meet men, and her type is the very aggressive businessman. Of course she tells Elliot this in a polite way, but what she really means is that Elliot is a nerd! Elliot responds that three women in the last month have told him the same thing and that he guesses the sensitive, artistic type is out of style. What's our best advice for Elliot? The same thing his mother has been telling him for twenty-five years: Stand up straight!

Quinn had an affair with Dirk for about a year. The relationship had its ups and downs, but the sex was always wonderful. Quinn was strongly attracted to Dirk from the moment she saw him, and every time they were together, she could hardly wait to go to bed with him. Dirk found Quinn exciting also, but he was a less physical person, preferring solitude and soul searching to stroking and sex.

One day, after several months of being out of touch, Quinn bumps into Dirk in a local restaurant. Both are waiting at the bar for a table. Spotting each other, they decide to catch up on news. At first they stand next to each other, each leaning an elbow on the bar, alternately laughing and being serious. They are warming up to each other all over again. Despite the fact that Quinn is mad at Dirk for not having called her for so long, she realizes that she is still attracted to him, for she is in touch with both her body and her emotions.

As the conversation progresses, their arms gradually move closer. Dirk brushes Quinn's arm with his hand, as though to make a point. Quinn touches his forehead, as if to push aside a stray hair. They lean closer to each other, ostensibly to hear better in the noisy bar. As they lean, their legs touch. At first each pulls his or her own leg away, but soon they touch again, and gradually they leave their legs together. Dirk reaches out and covers Quinn's hand with his own. As he looks into her eyes, they both recognize that they are incredibly turned on. They decide to forego the dinner and to head to Quinn's place.

This is a fairly straightforward example of the mating ritual, and though it is more pronounced because the two people have been lovers in the past and have an intimate feel for each other's bodies, this is the exact same process that occurs between people who may not have that familiarity. The more we like our partner, the more likely we are to lean toward him or her or to engage in casual touching, which is really a signal that we are willing to engage in more intimate touching with that individual. It's a precursor to actual sexual activity.

Shauna works as a secretary for Bill and Don, two young executives, both of whom depend on and admire her. They are quite competitive with each other, and each wants Shauna to consider herself more his secretary than the other's. Shauna is aware of—and amused by—this feud. She wishes that Bill, the unmarried one, would ask her out on a date, but so far he hasn't approached her.

One day Shauna is sitting in Don's office chatting with her boss. They are having a friendly conversation that has nothing at all to do with work. Bill walks by the door and notices the intimate and friendly scene. He walks in and stands next to Shauna, placing a firm hand on her shoulder in a casual way. "What's going on?" he asks. Don and Shauna reply that nothing is going on, just office goofing off. Shauna returns to her desk, smiling. She recognizes Bill's gesture for what it is—one of proprietorship. Bill is expressing a claim on Shauna. Later, he does decide to ask her out.

* * *

Sally and Miles are spending the evening together. They plan to order in Chinese food, watch television, and later make love. This is typical of many nights they have shared. It is early, though, so Sally is sitting on the floor, reading the paper and relaxing after a long, hard day. Miles takes the sports section and sits behind her, easing his back against her own. They relax companionably together, each using the other like a chair back and enjoying the proximity of their lover.

Later they make love and lie happily snuggled together. Sally turns on her side to fall asleep. Miles moves closer, fitting his body against hers in the popular spoon position. Then he wraps one arm over Sally's arms, one leg over Sally's legs. She is encased like a butterfly in a cocoon. Both sigh happily and fall asleep.

This is simple, uncomplicated, and very lovely body language. Sally and Miles both enjoy each other's physical presence and they are unashamed to reach for more closeness. This signifies an open and honest relationship in which both partners feel able to ask for and receive physical intimacy. That's a good sign of compatibility on other levels as well.

Lynn has recently been divorced. She was devastated when her husband left her and she has only agreed to date Mark because her best friend, Ellen, insisted on fixing them up as a way to cheer Lynn out of her depression.

When Mark arrives to pick Lynn up, she offers him a drink. They sit and chat while Mark drinks his wine. Lynn looks him over and finds him appealing. He is attractive, well groomed, and she enjoys talking with him. He seems to like her.

But Lynn is sitting almost sideways on the couch, with her body turned away from Mark and only her face aimed in his direction. Her legs are tightly crossed. Her arms are folded in front of her chest. She is in a visual knot, and although Mark does not consciously notice, it does affect him. No matter how well they seem to be getting along, Lynn is not open to Mark. She is communicating the fact that she is closed off to a physical relationship. She does like Mark, however, and there may be some change in the future. If Mark is really savvy, he may ask Lynn about her recent separation, and if she is honest enough to reply that she still feels really bruised about the whole event, then Mark will discover that he will have to be patient.

Lynn is wounded and needs time to recover, and that is the message that her turned body yet smiling face is conveying. Of course if Mark doesn't examine the whole message, he may subconsciously conclude that Lynn just doesn't like him, and then he might not call her again, despite the good rapport they have shared.

Alex and Reed have been out on a wonderful date. They shared laughter, good conversation, a delicious meal, an entertaining movie, and a companionable walk back to Alex's apartment. When they get there, both are reluctant to part. Alex is very attracted to Reed, but she feels that though she will want to sleep with him eventually, she isn't ready yet. That doesn't mean that she wants to say goodnight at the door, however, so she invites him up for a cup of coffee. Reed is delighted, hoping that she will let him spend the night. He is very attracted to Alex, and though he isn't in love with her—yet—it isn't too soon for him to be turned on.

They enter the apartment, and Alex flips on the lights. She heads into the kitchen and puts the water on to boil. Reed follows her and spins her around, reaching down for a deep, delicious kiss. Alex responds completely. Reed kisses her several more times, and in every kiss Alex is an equal partner. Finally, just when she is about to feel faint with desire for this delightful man, Alex breaks away, using the boiling water as an excuse. Reed watches her make the coffee and then follows her back to the living room. He sits on the large sofa. Alex sets the coffee down on a table and seats herself in a nearby chair. Reed sighs. He suspects that Alex is backing off, and he is right. She is sending him a message that she isn't willing to get any closer this evening. But her warm and willing kisses promise that eventually she will, because they made it clear that she is very attracted to Reed. She's just controlling the situation sensibly. Reed won't even have to examine the body language, for the unconscious message works perfectly. And his interest in Alex is in no way diminished.

Barbara has been dating Chad for several weeks. She has enjoyed the evenings, but she is not as interested in Chad romantically as he is in her. With each subsequent date Chad presses for more intimacy, which Barbara does not want. She realizes that she will either have to stop seeing him or put the relationship on a different footing. Barbara likes Chad as a friend, and that is why she has kept seeing him so far, but she just doesn't feel that sexual buzz that would make her want to expand the relationship.

One evening Chad insists that Barbara come out to dinner with him and his brother, whom Barbara has never met. She is hesitant, primarily because she doesn't want to lead Chad on, and also because she feels that agreeing to meet a family member is a serious step. But Chad insists.

At the restaurant they are seated in a large curving booth, and soon after they are seated, Roger arrives. Barbara takes one look at Roger and falls in love. In fact, there is instant chemistry for both of them. Roger, however, feels loyal to his brother despite his attraction to Barbara.

As the three sit talking, Chad keeps reaching for Barbara. First he takes her hand in his in a companionable way. Barbara removes it as subtly as possible, all the while continuing her dialogue with Roger. Chad puts one arm along the banquette, draping it over the back of Barbara's seat and eventually resting it on Barbara's shoulder. Barbara leans forward, removing her back from the booth, and Chad's hand falls off her shoulder. Meanwhile Roger has become aware of the situation between Barbara and Chad. He tells a joke to reduce the increasing tension. Barbara is focused completely on him, her eyes never leaving his for a minute. She leans toward Roger as she listens. Roger is cordial and friendly, but he remains upright.

This is a serious situation. Roger is not only aware of Barbara's interest in him, he returns her feelings, but his loyalty to his brother prevents him from responding, as shown by his upright stance. Barbara has given ample messages to Chad that she is not interested—and if he were paying attention, he would see that she prefers his brother, something he obviously doesn't want to face.

The problem is that Barbara has been sending messages of disinterest all along to Chad, but he is insensitive to her feelings. He simply wants her to gratify his own desires. And now Barbara probably won't get to date Roger, at least not until enough time has passed for Chad to get over her and to be willing to allow Roger to press his interest.

This is one situation where body language is not enough. Barbara will have to be honest with Chad and tell him that she likes him only as a friend.

Body language is there for all of us to read, if we are willing to do so and savvy enough to match the signals with the appropriate message. It's not all that difficult, really. Someone who looks relaxed and happy probably feels that way, and vice versa. Someone who is smiling and friendly looking may be congenial and friendly. And someone who leans toward you is more interested than someone who leans away. Take some time to examine the body language of the people around you (but those who are not interacting with you). Check out the couple at another table in a restaurant, or your co-workers. You'll be amazed at how quickly you are able to identify what is going on in the subtext simply through body language.

Then once you have been able to isolate emotions by virtue of their physical expression, use that knowledge. If you see a divinely attractive stranger across the room, look purposefully in his or her direction. Smile invitingly. Make eye contact. This could encourage that individual to come toward you for an introduction. If you want to let someone know you are available either emotionally or physically to him or her, lean toward that person during conversation. Smile your most winning smile. Reach out and touch if you are interested—your partner will get your message quickly enough. Many relationships have started between consciously unaware partners who simply responded to each other's natural urges to touch them casually during conversation. Body language is more natural and far more eloquent than the most flowerly love sonnet, and it is a lingo we all understand—whether we know it or not.

CHAPTER V

BIORHYTHMS

HAVE YOU EVER SAT BY THE SEASIDE AND watched the waves roar into the shore and bubble back to the depths of the sea again? If you think for a moment about the process you've witnessed, you'll realize that there is a pattern, a rhythm to the waves. They gather strength, they peak, they lose strength, they wane, they gather strength again. This is the cycle of the sea, and anyone observing the ocean's majesty will agree that it isn't just the beauty of the waves or even the marvelous smell of the sea that is so mesmerizing. It is the repetitive quality—the rhythm—that creates a hypnotic fascination.

We all respond to repeating rhythms, possibly because we, like the ocean, express our own life force in such repeating rhythms. Women know the rhythmic cycle concept only too intimately because of the monthly cycle of their own bodies. But there are other important cycles of which many people—men and women—are unaware. This is what biorhythms are all about.

Biorhythms chart three different cycles within the human body: a 23-day physical cycle, a 28-day sensitivity or emotional cycle, and a 33-day intellectual cycle. Just like the wave crashing to shore, these cycles build, peak, and wane, giving us all peak days and low days for each of the three categories. There are also critical days occurring in each cycle at the middle point where the energy has peaked in one direction and is starting to go in the other. These are called critical days because our bodies are in flux at such a time. Thus, on a physical critical day our reflexes are not as good, and we might be more likely to have an accident. On an emotional critical day we might feel all aflutter and find a calm state of mind exceedingly difficult to achieve. Arguments and emotional scenes are one possibility at such a time. On an intellectual critical day, we don't think as clearly and have a hard time making rational, objective decisions. Planning is also difficult.

It is important to understand that the scope of difference among days in any cycle is relatively small. On a peak physical day you are not likely to win a marathon; in the same way you're unlikely to be bedridden on a low physical day. Those are too extreme, but that is the assumption many of us have about peaks and lows. It is more realistic to assume that on a peak physical day you will be energized and outgoing to the maximum of your own potential. Thus, if you are a marathon runner, you might very well win a race. But if you are sedentary by nature, you're not likely even to enter one—whether you're peaking physically or not. You might just do something a little more physical than usual. Even on a low day, the marathon runner is still likely to be more active than the sedentary person. It's all a matter of degrees, and each reading is relative to the individual's own life-style.

Thus, you can see that your biorhythms form a useful barometer for the intimate workings of your own system—and your lover's. By knowing more about your energy cycles, you can take advantage of that knowledge for scheduling. For example, if you are planning a high physical activity, such as a marathon or perhaps a honeymoon, you wouldn't want to schedule it on a low physical day. If you are expecting—or making—a marriage proposal, you might want to wait until your intellectual cycle is at a high, so you can make a clear-headed decision rather than one based solely on emotions. Conversely, if you have a history of letting your head rule your heart, it might be better to choose a time period that maximizes the emotional and minimizes the intellectual. If you're scheduling a first date, a high intellectual and emotional score could help you converse more easily and make emotional connections more effectively than you might otherwise. After all, first dates are always stressful. If you note, for that same first date, that you are having a peak physical day, you might want to watch out, because on such a day you might be far more susceptible to sexual overtures and might thus begin an intimate relationship far earlier in the game than you had intended.

The first step in using your biorhythms is to have them calculated. If you enjoy doing mathematical things, there are a number of books available that will tell you how to do the calculations yourself. If you have a computer, there are several inexpensive programs available that will calculate the biorhythms for you. All you need is your birth date, or the birth date of the person whose biorhythms you wish to calculate. Another easy way to get your biorhythms is to order them from a computer printout firm. Many of these services are available everywhere. We recommend Astro Computing in San Diego—they're accurate, speedy, and inexpensive. One year's worth of biorhythms costs under $5. Write to Astro Computing at P.O. Box 16430, San Diego, CA 92116. Or call them at (619)-297-92203.

Now let's look at Jennifer's biorhythms and learn how to read them. First you will notice a listing of days. This is the basis for biorhythms, which are calculated day by day from the date of birth. If you ever wanted to brag about your age in terms of the number of days you've been alive, this is your chance! On the other side of the biorhythm curve is the current date, indicating the specific biorhythms for the date in question.

There are also daily listings for amplitude and cycle for each of the three categories: physical, emotional, and intellectual. Amplitude describes the relative strength or weakness of that particular cycle. A +100 percent amplitude is the highest peak of energy; a −100 percent amplitude is the lowest level of energy. A 0 percent amplitude represents a critical day, one in which the energy of that particular cycle is in flux—going from positive to negative or negative to positive. Generally speaking, these critical days occur at the beginning and the mid-point of every cycle. Thus, not every critical day will be marked with a zero percent.

The cycle listing indicates where Jennifer is in each of her three cycles. They move along day by day until the cycle is completed. The physical cycle has twenty-three

JENNIFER

BIRTH DATE = 9 6 1964

```
AGE                 I=INTELLECTUAL                                   AMPLITUDE        CYCLE
(DAYS)     P=PHYSICAL       E=SENSITIVITY      DAY   DATE       %PH   %SE   %IN   23 28 33

8638 .I         P     E                . SUN  5- 1-88   -40     0  -100   14 15 26
8639 .I     P     E   .                . MON  5- 2-88   -63   -22   -97   15 16 27
8640 . I P     E      .                . TUE  5- 3-88   -82   -43   -91   16 17 28
8641 . P I  E         .                . WED  5- 4-88   -94   -62   -81   17 18 29
8642 .P  E I          .                . THU  5- 5-88  -100   -78   -69   18 19 30
8643 .P E    I        .                . FRI  5- 6-88   -98   -90   -54   19 20 31
8644 .E P       I     .                . SAT  5- 7-88   -89   -97   -37   20 21 32
8645 .E   P        I  .                . SUN  5- 8-88   -73  -100   -19   21 22 33
8646 .E       P       I                . MON  5- 9-88   -52   -97     0   22 23  1
8647 .  E         P   .  I             . TUE  5-10-88   -27   -90    19   23 24  2
8648 .   E            P     I          . WED  5-11-88     0   -78    37    1 25  3
8649 .      E         .   P    I       . THU  5-12-88    27   -62    54    2 26  4
8650 .         E      .       P  I     . FRI  5-13-88    52   -43    69    3 27  5
8651 .            E   .           PI   . SAT  5-14-88    73   -22    81    4 28  6
8652 .                E             PI . SUN  5-15-88    89     0    91    5  1  7
8653 .                .   E           P. MON  5-16-88    98    22    97    6  2  8
8654 .                .      E        P. TUE  5-17-88   100    43   100    7  3  9
8655 .                .         E    PI. WED  5-18-88    94    62    99    8  4 10
8656 .                .            P I . THU  5-19-88    82    78    95    9  5 11
8657 .                .         P   E  . FRI  5-20-88    63    90    87   10  6 12
8658 .                .     P     I   E. SAT  5-21-88    40    97    76   11  7 13
8659 .                . P       I     E. SUN  5-22-88    14   100    62   12  8 14
8660 .              P .      I        E. MON  5-23-88   -14    97    46   13  9 15
8661 .          P     .    I        E  . TUE  5-24-88   -40    90    28   14 10 16
8662 .      P         . I          E   . WED  5-25-88   -63    78    10   15 11 17
8663 .   P          I .         E      . THU  5-26-88   -82    62   -10   16 12 18
8664 . P         I    .      E         . FRI  5-27-88   -94    43   -28   17 13 19
8665 .P        I      .   E            . SAT  5-28-88  -100    22   -46   18 14 20
8666 .P     I         E                . SUN  5-29-88   -98     0   -62   19 15 21
8667 .  P I       E   .                . MON  5-30-88   -89   -22   -76   20 16 22
8668 .  I P    E      .                . TUE  5-31-88   -73   -43   -87   21 17 23
8669 . I    E P       .                . WED  6- 1-88   -52   -62   -95   22 18 24
8670 .I  E        P   .                . THU  6- 2-88   -27   -78   -99   23 19 25
8671 .I E             P                . FRI  6- 3-88     0   -90  -100    1 20 26
8672 .E               .   P            . SAT  6- 4-88    27   -97   -97    2 21 27
8673 .EI              .       P        . SUN  6- 5-88    52  -100   -91    3 22 28
8674 .E  I            .           P    . MON  6- 6-88    73   -97   -81    4 23 29
8675 .  E  I          .             P  . TUE  6- 7-88    89   -90   -69    5 24 30
8676 .   E   I        .               P. WED  6- 8-88    98   -78   -54    6 25 31
8677 .      E   I     .               P. THU  6- 9-88   100   -62   -37    7 26 32
8678 .         E   I  .              P . FRI  6-10-88    94   -43   -19    8 27 33
8679 .            E   I            P   . SAT  6-11-88    82   -22     0    9 28  1
8680 .                E  I      P      . SUN  6-12-88    63     0    19   10  1  2
8681 .                .   E P          . MON  6-13-88    40    22    37   11  2  3
8682 .                . P    E I       . TUE  6-14-88    14    43    54   12  3  4
8683 .              P .         EI     . WED  6-15-88   -14    62    69   13  4  5
8684 .          P     .            E   . THU  6-16-88   -40    78    81   14  5  6
8685 .      P         .             EI . FRI  6-17-88   -63    90    91   15  6  7
8686 .   P            .               E. SAT  6-18-88   -82    97    97   16  7  8
8687 . P              .               E. SUN  6-19-88   -94   100   100   17  8  9
8688 .P               .               E. MON  6-20-88  -100    97    99   18  9 10
8689 .P               .             EI . TUE  6-21-88   -98    90    95   19 10 11
8690 .  P             .            EI  . WED  6-22-88   -89    78    87   20 11 12
8691 .    P           .         E I    . THU  6-23-88   -73    62    76   21 12 13
8692 .        P       .      E  I      . FRI  6-24-88   -52    43    62   22 13 14
8693 .            P   .   E  I         . SAT  6-25-88   -27    22    46   23 14 15
8694 .                P    I           . SUN  6-26-88     0     0    28    1 15 16
8695 .            E   . I P            . MON  6-27-88    27   -22    10    2 16 17
8696 .         E    I .       P        . TUE  6-28-88    52   -43   -10    3 17 18
8697 .      E    I    .           P    . WED  6-29-88    73   -62   -28    4 18 19
8698 .   E     I      .             P  . THU  6-30-88    89   -78   -46    5 19 20
8699 .  E   I         .               P. FRI  7- 1-88    98   -90   -62    6 20 21
8700 .E   I           .               P. SAT  7- 2-88   100   -97   -76    7 21 22
8701 .E I             .              P . SUN  7- 3-88    94  -100   -87    8 22 23
8702 .EI              .            P   . MON  7- 4-88    82   -97   -95    9 23 24
8703 .I E             .         P      . TUE  7- 5-88    63   -90   -99   10 24 25
8704 .I  E            .     P          . WED  7- 6-88    40   -78  -100   11 25 26
8705 .I     E         . P              . THU  7- 7-88    14   -62   -97   12 26 27
8706 . I       E    P .                . FRI  7- 8-88   -14   -43   -91   13 27 28
8707 .   I      P E   .                . SAT  7- 9-88   -40   -22   -81   14 28 29
```

days and then goes back to one. We can use those figures to calculate the mid-points, or critical days. In the twenty-three-day physical cycle, the first critical day occurs at day one, or on Jennifer's biorhythms, Wednesday, May 11. We divide twenty-three by two to figure out the mid-point, which is between eleven and twelve. Thus that becomes a second critical day in that cycle.

As we look at the actual graph of Jennifer's biorhythms, this does begin to make sense. Day one of the physical cycle, a critical day, shows the P—the symbol for the physical curve—crossing the center dividing line. That line represents the zero point, where positive and negative meet. The P symbol moves steadily upward, getting stronger and stronger, indicating a time of physical peaking. The physical cycle peaks, reaching +100 percent amplitude on May 17. From there the energy starts to wane, going down to a critical day once again in mid-cycle, between May 22 and 23, or eleven or twelve days after the cycle began on May 11.

Biorhythm graphs are extremely easy to read. Above zero is positive, below zero is less positive, and zero is critical. It's that simple! Now let's take this information and make sense of it as it applies to real life.

Let's check back with Jennifer to see what actually happened on some of the days listed in her biorhythms. On Wednesday, May 18, she was peaking both physically and intellectually. On that day she arrived at work early, after taking a brisk walk rather than using public transportation. She just felt like using her body more than usual, something that is quite natural on physical days. She was also on an intellectual high, and since her work requires quite a bit of intellectual participation, she was ready, willing, and able to get going. She attended a meeting early in the day, which she remembers because there was some lively discussion. Jennifer disagreed with a number of her coworkers on a specific issue and was able to persuade them to her point of view, using savvy reasoning and a dynamic means of self-expression.

She took an extra long lunch hour, because the day was so lovely that she decided to attend one of the popular lunchtime concerts at a nearby office building. While she was tapping her toe to the rhythm of the music, Jim spotted her and was entranced. He came over, introduced himself, and they made a date to have dinner later in the week. Jennifer returned to work, received a phone call from an old friend, and made plans to go to a happy hour after work.

That night, Jennifer was the life of the party, dancing with many different guys and enjoying herself immensely. Several of the men she met took her phone number and promised to call. By the time Jennifer got home, she should have been exhausted, but she wasn't, so she stayed up late reading before bed. This is typical of such a high energy day. These are the days when we frequently meet new lovers, new friends, or go out looking for fun.

On Monday, May 23, Jennifer got together with Jim for their first date. She was having a high emotional day. Her physical cycle, so high when she met Jim, was now at a critical point, and in fact Jennifer had to run to the store to buy new pantyhose because she had bumped her leg rather badly on her desk at work, tearing her nylons in the process. Her intellectual cycle was still high, but on the down swing.

She and Jim established an amazing rapport. They

could talk about everything, but the real communication was happening below the surface. They each had a sense of the other's essence, not just the superficial details that usually form immediate impressions. They lingered over dinner, then Jim suggested taking Jennifer to a favorite dance spot, and they spent hours there, requesting slow numbers for romantic dances while the disco crowd booed and asked for the latest from Michael Jackson. Jim, who was having a peak physical day, wanted Jennifer to spend the night with him, but she felt that it was too soon. They decided to walk to her home, despite the fact that a light ran had begun to fall. They walked together talking and enjoying the intimacy of the evening and the quiet rain. It seemed like the beginning of something special. The next morning, as Jennifer's physical rhythms were going even father down, she awoke feeling tired and achey. Her nose began to run. Oh, no! She had caught a cold from her night of romance and her walk in the rain. All her energies were on the downswing by then, but a day or two in bed dreaming of her newly begun romance with Jim helped her to release the cold germs.

Over the next few weeks, Jim took Jennifer out several times, and they both began to fall in love. By Thursday, June 9, Jennifer had decided she was ready to be intimate with Jim on their next date—just in time to coincide with a peak in her physical cycle. He, in the middle of an emotional peak, decided to propose to her. Needless to say, there was a happy ending.

Although we all have peaks in every cycle every month, we all don't fall in love monthly—at least most of us don't. This is simply an example of a romance coinciding with a biorhythmic peak cycle. You can have your own biorhythms calculated for important times—both positive and negative—in your own past and search for energy patterns that may have influenced your behavior or decisions on those occasions. That way you can maximize the positive energies in the future.

Stephanie decided to do just that. She had noticed that every time she met a new lover, she was having some kind of peak. Interestingly, it wasn't always in the same cycle. She met Ryan and Stan during physical peaks, and she had torrid affairs with both of them; she met Dave and Alex during peak emotional times, and she was head over heels in love with each of them; and she met Chad and Sam during intellectual peaks—they had great rapport. It seemed as though the relationships themselves reflected what was going on in her biorhythms, and that is very logical to assume. The experience Stephanie sought and received was directed by her inner needs as determined by the flow of her own internal energies. On high physical days she needed physical contact and was sending out sexy physical vibrations. On high emotional days, she was looking for an emotional connection with someone with whom she could share the sensitive side of her nature and who would respond in an open and emotionally intimate way. And on intellectual days, she wanted mental stimulation. It makes a lot of sense.

Stephanie wanted to take advantage of this information, so she had her biorhythms charted for a year. She noted when her peak days occurred and decided in advance to go out whenever any of her cycles peaked. Thus, she was increasing her chances of meeting new men by making sure that she was out where the men could find her, instead of staying home alone at such a time. On the physically high days, she certainly had the energy to get out and go! At those times she would do something physical, such as going for a walk, taking a golf lesson, or heading to the gym for a workout and a swim. On peak emotional days, she might wander through a mall—in the men's departments—or take in a movie or an art exhibit. On peak intellectual days, she could browse through a bookstore, attend a play or a lecture, or sign up for a class in something that would not only interest her, but might also attract interesting men. Once Stephanie got her biorhythms charted and discovered her peak days, she was never alone again.

Often more than one cycle will peak at the same time. If you look back to Jennifer's biorhythms, you will notice that all three cycles peak together part of the time, but the emotional and intellectual factors seem closely allied all of the time. This is an indication of a period in which these energies function together. In fact, Jennifer frequently uses words to express emotions, and she also helps other people to better express their own feelings through her work. Closely linked intellectual and emotional cycles are a boost to a creative individual. When more than one cycle peaks at the same time, the energy is heightened because the person in question will demand stimulation in all the peak areas, rather than completely focused stimulation in just one area.

Some people have cycles that are very connected, flowing together more often than not. Look at Eric's graph. Notice how all three of his curves flow similarly. Obviously this will not happen all of the time, because of the difference in the length of each cycle. When the curves flow together, it is an indication of a very focused person, one who uses all of his various energies to-

ERIC

BIRTH DATE = 4 14 1949

```
 AGE              I=INTELLECTUAL                                       AMPLITUDE        CYCLE
(DAYS)      P=PHYSICAL     E=SENSITIVITY      DAY    DATE       %PH    %SE    %IN   23 28 33

14241 .      E     I   .              P  . SUN  4-10-88     89    -62    -28    5 18 19
14242 .   E     I      .                P. MON  4-11-88     98    -78    -46    6 19 20
14243 .  E   I         .                P. TUE  4-12-88    100    -90    -62    7 20 21
14244 .E   I           .               P . WED  4-13-88     94    -97    -76    8 21 22
14245 .E I             .             P   . THU  4-14-88     82   -100    -87    9 22 23
14246 .EI              .          P      . FRI  4-15-88     63    -97    -95   10 23 24
14247 .I E             .      P          . SAT  4-16-88     40    -90    -99   11 24 25
14248 .I  E            . P               . SUN  4-17-88     14    -78   -100   12 25 26
14249 .I     E       P .                 . MON  4-18-88    -14    -62    -97   13 26 27
14250 . I       EP     .                 . TUE  4-19-88    -40    -43    -91   14 27 28
14251 .   I  P     E   .                 . WED  4-20-88    -63    -22    -81   15 28 29
14252 .   P I          E                 . THU  4-21-88    -82      0    -69   16  1 30
14253 . P     I        .    E            . FRI  4-22-88    -94     22    -54   17  2 31
14254 .P         I     .       E         . SAT  4-23-88   -100     43    -37   18  3 32
14255 .P            I  .          E      . SUN  4-24-88    -98     62    -19   19  4 33
14256 .  P             I             E   . MON  4-25-88    -89     78      0   20  5  1
14257 .    P           .   I          E  . TUE  4-26-88    -73     90     19   21  6  2
14258 .        P       .      I         E. WED  4-27-88    -52     97     37   22  7  3
14259 .            P   .         I      E. THU  4-28-88    -27    100     54   23  8  4
14260 .                P           I    E. FRI  4-29-88      0     97     69    1  9  5
14261 .                .    P        IE  . SAT  4-30-88     27     90     81    2 10  6
14262 .                .        P    E I . SUN  5- 1-88     52     78     91    3 11  7
14263 .                .          E P   I. MON  5- 2-88     73     62     97    4 12  8
14264 .                .       E      P I. TUE  5- 3-88     89     43    100    5 13  9
14265 .                .    E           P. WED  5- 4-88     98     22     99    6 14 10
14266 .                E               IP. THU  5- 5-88    100      0     95    7 15 11
14267 .            E   .              IP . FRI  5- 6-88     94    -22     87    8 16 12
14268 .         E      .            IP   . SAT  5- 7-88     82    -43     76    9 17 13
14269 .      E         .          P      . SUN  5- 8-88     63    -62     62   10 18 14
14270 .   E            .      PI         . MON  5- 9-88     40    -78     46   11 19 15
14271 .  E             . P   I           . TUE  5-10-88     14    -90     28   12 20 16
14272 .E             P . I               . WED  5-11-88    -14    -97     10   13 21 17
14273 .E         P   I .                 . THU  5-12-88    -40   -100    -10   14 22 18
14274 .E     P    I    .                 . FRI  5-13-88    -63    -97    -28   15 23 19
14275 .  EP     I      .                 . SAT  5-14-88    -82    -90    -46   16 24 20
14276 . P E  I         .                 . SUN  5-15-88    -94    -78    -62   17 25 21
14277 .P   I E         .                 . MON  5-16-88   -100    -62    -76   18 26 22
14278 .P I      E      .                 . TUE  5-17-88    -98    -43    -87   19 27 23
14279 . IP         E   .                 . WED  5-18-88    -89    -22    -95   20 28 24
14280 .I   P           E                 . THU  5-19-88    -73      0    -99   21  1 25
14281 .I       P       .    E            . FRI  5-20-88    -52     22   -100   22  2 26
14282 .I           P   .       E         . SAT  5-21-88    -27     43    -97   23  3 27
14283 . I              P          E      . SUN  5-22-88      0     62    -91    1  4 28
14284 .   I            .    P        E   . MON  5-23-88     27     78    -81    2  5 29
14285 .     I          .        P     E  . TUE  5-24-88     52     90    -69    3  6 30
14286 .       I        .            P   E. WED  5-25-88     73     97    -54    4  7 31
14287 .          I     .              P E. THU  5-26-88     89    100    -37    5  8 32
14288 .             I  .                P. FRI  5-27-88     98     97    -19    6  9 33
14289 .                I              E P. SAT  5-28-88    100     90      0    7 10  1
14290 .                .   I         E P . SUN  5-29-88     94     78     19    8 11  2
14291 .                .      I   E  P   . MON  5-30-88     82     62     37    9 12  3
```

gether most of the time. This is Eric's nature, and such a cycle feels quite normal. High energy is part of his intellectual approach, and a dynamic passion is part of his emotional makeup. One cycle does not really compete with another for prominence; rather they all combine to make Eric very centered in his every action and sure on every level of what he is doing. In this extremely focused energy cycle, he will experience an important time in which he must deal with lots of different issues in a very cohesive way. Decisions made now will affect all areas of his life. But because all systems are functioning together, such a time will be less stressful than it might otherwise be.

Sharon broke up with Stan after a long and unsatisfying relationship. There was just no passion and no pizzazz. It wasn't that Stan was boring, but rather that they had no mutual chemistry. Sharon was never in the mood when Stan wanted to make love. And whenever she was feeling torrid, he wasn't home. Despite the fact that they had fair communication and compatible values, there was simply not enough passion to keep them together.

When Sharon discovered biorhythms, she noticed something interesting. Her own biorhythms and those of Stan were incredibly at odds. When she was up, he was down—all the time. Of course that was not startling news, since that was why they broke up. But the biorhythms made sense of it. No wonder they were so incompatible physically—they were incompatible physically! Their physical cycles were completely opposite. Sharon learned one of the unfortunate truths about biorhythms—we all feel far more compatible with someone whose biorhythms are similar to our own. When internal rhythms are reinforced by those of a mate, it is a lot easier to get along harmoniously.

Sharon decided to look for men whose biorhythms matched her own. Since she has a personal computer and the software necessary to run biorhythms, it was no big deal to ask a guy's birth date and to run out his chart before the first date.

That was how she met Steven. It was love—or, as Sharon likes to describe it, lust—at first sight. Even before she learned Steven's birth date, she was in the throes of a passionate obsession. In fact, it was three days before she could tear herself away from Steven and the bedroom to run his biorhythms on the computer. But once she did, she learned the obvious: They had exactly matching physical cycles. That was good news for the future of their sexual relationship, since it implied that both parties would be likely to feel desire at the same time. It in no way described their basic attraction to each other, however. Biorhythms cannot predict that. We can come to the likely conclusion, however, that since a potential for an attraction between Sharon and Steven existed all along, their corresponding physical peaks on their first date were responsible for the urgency of their passion. Of course if Sharon later discovers that she and Steven have little in common besides the hots, she may decide to look elsewhere for a more suitable mate—one who can satisfy her on all levels. Biorhythms won't tell her where to look or what to expect from a specific partner. All they can give her is the gauge of his relative energy levels in the three areas described.

What if you discover that your lover's biorhythms are at odds with your own? Does that mean that you have to divorce or break up with him or her and go looking for your biorhythmic twin? Of course not! As we said already, biorhythms can't predict the potential for attraction or true compatibility within a relationship. They simply measure energy levels and the energy compatibility.

So what can you do? First examine the charts. If you discover that one partner has a physical peak when the other's physical energies are plummeting, does that mean there will never be any sex? Only if you choose to handle it that way. There are other possibilities. If the high physical partner really wants sex and the other isn't excited, you could decide that the aroused partner should take the lead. It is his or her responsibility to do everything possible to turn the other partner on. All that individual has to do is relax and be willing to respond. Chances are that eventually both of you will be in the mood for love, even if it takes a little longer. After all, one of you is only at a physical low, not dead!

You could also use your biorhythm charts to determine the times when your energy intersects most positively. If Joe is just coming down from his peak and Jane is starting to rise out of her low, perhaps they could decide to meet somewhere in the middle. If scheduling a time for sex seems like the epitome of unromantic, then pretend you are single and call it a date. The magic will return. You can also cut each other some slack. During Joe's peak, he can go out for some vigorous exercise while Jane enjoys her low in a bubble bath at home. By the time they meet for dinner, Joe will need less of a physical release, and Jane will have stored up her energy. The whole point is to show understanding, love, and sensitivity to the other person. That is what makes successful unions, and biorhythms can be a helpful tool to develop such understanding.

Another way to use your biorhythms to help create a smoothly functioning partnership is by being aware of each other's critical days. Suppose Joe is having a critical emotional day, and he feels all itchy and temperamental. If both he and Jane are aware of this fact, they can understand when he is cross, or complains of being neglected. She, on the other hand, can simply forgive him his outbursts without letting her feelings get hurt and participating in an emotional argument that is without a real foundation. If one partner is having a critical intellectual day, he or she can seek advice and guidance from the partner who is all clear. Or they can decide to postpone any major decisions they have to make singly or together.

It seems that most people who have successful relationships do so because of a high degree of acceptance of each other. They don't place unreasonable demands on each other, and each allows the other to express himself or herself without fear of reprisal. A knowledge of biorhythms can foster this kind of cooperative spirit. If your mate is on an intellectual high and feeling talky, and wants to tell you the particulars of his or her hobby that wouldn't interest you even on a good day—or a desert island—don't say, "I can't possibly follow you, dear, I'm too stupid today to comprehend even the television page. See—here are my biorhythms!" Treat your lover with the courtesy you would offer a stranger—relax and listen. If you're having an intellectual low, you're *not* stupid, unless you started out that way! Use intellectual low time to enjoy other people's ideas. Flashes of inspiration usually come during the peak days.

The main use of biorhythms—within relationships or not—is to make you more aware of the subtle fluctuations of energy within your own system. You can use them like a planning device, scheduling important events during peak times. But don't get so hooked on your biorhythms that you're afraid to leave the bed on low days. That is a gross misrepresentation of their use. Only people who suffer from psychic disorders such as manic-depression have such widely fluctuating mood swings. Yours, like those of most other people, will be much milder. Some days you will feel ready to set the world on fire and on others you will prefer to watch while somebody else strikes the match.

We all participate in the universal ebb and flow of energies, for all of life is like the process of taking a breath—drawing in, holding a while, and releasing. Unless you're holding your breath or hyperventilating, each breath is very similar to each other, and so is each day of life rather like every other. Yes, there are days of extreme happiness and deep sadness, wild exuberance and mild depression, but it is always important to keep these matters in perspective. Use your biorhythms as a tool to understand your own nature more precisely, but don't overdo it. Never use your biorhythms as an excuse for failing to participate in life. Don't assume that your lover left you because of a low in biorhythms—yours or your lover's. Life just doesn't work that way. Of course, if you're an astronaut, it might be better to avoid shuttling to the moon on a triple low day or on a critical day. But if you're a housewife, don't use a physical low as an excuse for not being able to go to the market for a quart of milk!

Biorhythms are best when used positively to help you with elective activities. If you have a choice about when to schedule something, choose the most positive date according to your biorhythms. In that way you are taking this tool of science and letting it give you more of the one essential ingredient in your life—the power to create your own reality most positively according to your own desires, wishes, and hopes.

CHAPTER VI

tea leaves

NOBODY KNOWS EXACTLY HOW PEOPLE started reading tea leaves, but this legend may recount the beginning of the art of tasseography, as it is called.

Centuries ago, in the rugged Asian wilderness, the Princess Su-Lan was dragged away from her father's caravan by a band of roving Mongols. The fierce warrior who ruled the vast, sandy plain eyed his beautiful captive with more interest than he gave her father's jewels. Thus began a love affair that today is legend. Ensconced in a palace built for her by a thousand slaves, Su-Lan enchanted her savage. He watched trancelike as her slender fingers added, bit by bit, the ingredients for the magic tea she brewed daily.

Ginseng, roots of licorice, ginger, lovage, and chicory gave their essences to Su-Lan's kettle. She sifted rose hips and bits of orange peel and gently dropped them into the steaming waters. A few perfect blackberry leaves floated on the surface of the tea, and the lush fragrance of cinnamon filled the air. The Mongol inhaled the scent and took deep comfort at the sight of his beauty tending her teapot.

Every day she brewed the tea, and as the weathered warrior drank the fragrant brew, Su-Lan offered gentle suggestions about changes within his domain. Then the Mongol would pass his empty cup to Su-Lan and she would read his destiny. Each day his reputation and his successes grew because of her advice and her insights.

Whether or not this is a true story, there is little doubt that the art of tea reading developed in a similar fashion. In ancient times there was great store set on symbols, because early man—and woman—wanted as much advice about future destinies as we do now—probably more, because in those days there was a greater potential for disaster. Thus, wise people would study the many symbols that surrounded them, and each simple part of nature, such as an animal or a tree, would have certain qualities attributed to it as part of the lore of deciphering the mysteries of the universe. These symbols evolved through time and experience, with experienced seers passing on information to the next generation of mystics. Those who consulted the images in their cups, whether from tea leaves or coffee grounds, did so to gain important information about the future.

Today we tend to view those symbols with a great deal of skepticism. Can an acorn always mean success? But it would seem that it does, for the art of tea reading has provided valuable insight for such a long time that there must be a lot to it. Tea leaf readings are meant as a predictive tool, and though some of what they predict can be used for insight into current behavior patterns, the readings are not really intended to give that kind of guidance. Unlike the runes or the Tarot, both of which can be powerful psychological tools, tea leaves simply predict future events and occurrences.

The first step in doing your own readings is, of course, to stop drinking tea made from a tea bag. Get loose tea, because that is the only way to have leaves at the bottom of the cup. Then make sure that you have a tea cup with a classic bowl shape rather than the modern square-looking mug. Brew your tea, either in a pot by pouring boiling water over the loose tea and then pouring the brew into one or several cups, or by doing the same thing with a single cup. A tea pot is probably better, because you will have fewer leaves per cup and thus a less dense collection of leaves at the bottom. You must drink your own tea, for pouring the tea and then emptying the cup doesn't work as well. The rhythm of lifting the cup to your lips and emptying it gradually is how the patterns that will foretell your own future are created.

The second step requires a quantum leap of imagination out of the current video mentality and back into the symbol-reading nature of ages past. It's hard to look at a mass of leaves at the bottom of a cup and discern any images at all. Of course—you're too busy looking for the focus button as you would on your television set. Forget that! Tea leaves require the opposite of precision viewing. The images are supposed to be a little spacey, and so are you! Let your mind wander. Remember gazing at clouds and describing their shapes? That's the idea. First look at the bottom of the cup, not to scrutinize, but simply to let the patterns it contains register in your unconscious. Then close your eyes or look away.

You'll receive several quick impressions of the images in the cup. You'll be surprised at how quickly this will happen.

Once you have discerned the images that have appeared in your cup, make a list of them, or if you have a good memory, keep them in your mind. Then turn to the symbols glossary at the end of this chapter and interpret your symbols. The trick is to combine the meanings so that you get a coherent reading based on the group of symbols that have appeared to you. That is the best technique to use in any kind of psychic work. Always try to synthesize symbols and their meanings so that you get a whole message rather than a group of disjointed predictions.

Let's look at a sample reading to see how it is done.

Sherry was very enthusiastic about having her tea leaves read. She had just broken up with her boyfriend and was wondering if she should take him back. She prepared a pot of tea. Then she sat and enjoyed the steaming drink. Finally she was ready to look in the bottom of her cup. At first she couldn't recognize any symbols because it looked like a murky mass of stuff rather than a group of pictures. Sherry was determined to succeed, however, so she followed our advice, first staring at the cup in a spacey way and then looking off into the distance. Sure enough, she realized that she had seen the following symbols: a fern, an airplane, a bee, a daisy, and a ring.

One by one, Sherry looked up the meanings of the symbols. The fern is an indication of an unfaithful lover. Sherry gasped because although she had suspected that her ex-boyfriend had cheated on her, she had never been sure until now. The airplane is a sign of travel, and

Sherry did indeed have a vacation coming up soon. Another meaning for the airplane could be an emotional journey—away from the boyfriend in her past. The bee is a symbol of social activity, and this seemed to imply that Sherry would be meeting many new people, some of whom could become friends and some even romantic partners. The daisy is a sign of romantic happiness—a new lover will probably be coming into Sherry's life. And finally, the ring is a symbol of an approaching marriage. It would seem that Sherry has a lot of romance and fun in her future, and that's just what she was hoping for.

We can make sense of this reading as a whole by combining these very compatible symbols into a coherent message. The tea leaves seem to be telling Sherry that she has to release—or fly away from—her ties to the past: the unfaithful lover. When she does that, her life will change for the better, and new people will bring her happiness and pleasure.

This is an excellent scenario, one even a novice tea leaf reader could interpret. It always helps to know something about the person for whom you are doing the reading. For example, if we hadn't known about the breakup with the old boyfriend, we might have thought that Sherry was going to meet a new lover who would be unfaithful, or worse yet, that she herself would commit some form of infidelity while on vacation that could ruin her happy relationship. These are all possible interpretations of this reading.

Doing readings for yourself should be relatively uncomplicated, since you know your own life and history. Do play around with the symbols, however, so that you get the most logical chain of meaning and thereby come up with the best conclusion. When reading for friends or lovers, be sure to engage in a dialogue, because that is the best way to make real sense of anything psychic. All the information is individualized, and you must be sure that you are applying it in the most logical way possible to the individual at hand. Patience, affection, and a gentle spirit of understanding are your best tools in becoming a talented tea leaf reader.

TEA LEAF GLOSSARY OF SYMBOLS

Acorn Improvement of the current situation to the point of success

Airplane A trip. The success and safety of the trip depends on the condition of the plane.

Angel Fortunate news coming to you

Apple Money or success in business

Arrow A disappointment is likely.

Basket Can be wonderful news, success or money if full; the reverse if empty

Bee Social activities with new friends

Bird's Nest Happy marriage or true love

Bouquet Romance leading to true love

Bow or bow & arrow Gossip or trouble forthcoming

Box If open, your love life will improve. If closed, something lost will reappear.

Bracelet A forthcoming marriage

Branch A leafy branch is positive, bringing good news; without leaves, problems and disappointments are indicated.

Car Good luck, also travel—see airplane

Cat Someone you trust may betray you (unless you are a cat lover and are getting a pet).

Cherries Romance leading to true love

Clouds Future issues are uncertain. Check for problems—possibly financial.

Crab Beware of hidden enemies.

Crescent You'll be taking a trip.

Crown Good luck resulting from hard work; awards

Daffodil Joy and harmony in your life

Daisy Romance leading to true love

Devil Who surrounds you? Be careful of others.

Dog Friendly social activities with trusted allies

Eagle Improvements in your life

Egg Money and success

Elephant Rewards for the proper course; loyalty

Envelope Fortunate news coming to you

Eye Being more aware to solve problems.

Feather Need to focus more on your life

Fern Your lover may be cheating on you.

Fish Money and success plus great joy, abundance

Flower You'll get what you want in this matter.

Fruit More money will come to you.

Garland A promotion, more success, an award

Grapes Pleasure and joy in life

Gun Fights and arguments

Hammer Need to change your course in life

Hand New friends coming into your life

Harp True love with a congenial mate

Hat A change in life-style, possibly a new job

Hawk Avoid jealousy that could jeopardize your relationship.

Heart Romance, love, possible marriage

Heather Luck, money, success

Holly Timing device—important news in winter

Iceberg Look below surface for hidden dangers.

Initials People you know or new people in your life

Ivy leaf Trustworthy friend

Jewelry You'll receive a gift.

Kangaroo Happiness at home

Kettle If high up, happiness at home; if low, the reverse

Kite Your dreams will be realized if you're careful.

Knife A breakup within a romantic relationship

Ladder A promotion to a better position in life

Leaf Money, success, good luck

Necklace Potential romance with new partners, either through new beginnings or after a breakup

Numbers Timing device—number of days or months until an event described by other symbols

Oak Money and prosperity, good luck

Owl Things are not working out—change course to avoid failure.

Palm tree Romantic happiness; success at work

Peacock Money, success, luxury

Pear Success, prosperity, no worries about money

Question mark Be careful, go slowly.

Rainbow Happiness and luck in all areas

Rat Disloyalty surrounding you

Ring Possibility of marriage. The cleaner looking the image, the more happiness indicated.

Scissors Quarrels with a spouse, possible breakup

Shamrock You'll get your wish.

Snake Be cautious around those you don't trust.

Spoon A gift from a loving helper

Squirrel Success at last

Star Usually happiness, luck, and success

Swan Happiness and peace of mind

Telephone Communication—get on top of things.

Tree Improvements in general circumstances

Triangle Surprise news of success if pointing up, of failure if pointing down

Unicorn An elopement

Waterfall More money in your life

Wheel Money coming to you, depending on the completeness of the image

Wheelbarrow Reunion with someone from your past

CHAPTER VII

OUIJA BOARD

PAT MET STEVE BECAUSE OF A OUIJA BOARD. She was in a terrible quandary over her boyfriend Roger and she was hoping to get some significant answers from a Ouija board. After all, her mother had been holding weekly seances with her board for several years. Roger, on the other hand, thought the whole thing was a good excuse for a joke. He liked to say that Pat's mom had nagged her father for forty years while he was alive, and now she used her Ouija board so that she could make contact with him—and keep on nagging—now that he was no longer living.

That is the lore of the Ouija board—that it is able to act as a bridge between the spirit world and life on earth. Many people believe that the spirits of their dearly departed surround them and that through the Ouija board they can continue to make contact. This may or may not be true. Most people schooled in metaphysics believe that life is never over, that death is not an end but rather a transition, and also that people recently dead do stay around those they love for a while. But then the dead move on to do other things and to learn the lessons of their own path of evolution. Does that mean that there are no other spirits available? Certainly not! We all have a number of spirit guides who stay around us as helpers, teachers, and sometimes even muses. These spirits are much better sources of information, because they are really in touch with the events that surround each of us and they are here to help.

Pat had learned some of this information in her psychic development classes, and so she wanted to use the Ouija board both as a tool to get information about her love life and as a device for enhancing her own psychic abilities. Steve had similar aims.

Pat and Steve bumped heads in the toy store as both were reaching for the one and only Ouija board in stock. Being a gentleman, Steve insisted that Pat take the board. He even offered graciously to buy it for her. A modern, independent woman, Pat accepted the gesture, but paid for the board herself. As they stood in line at the cashier, they exchanged information about the Ouija board and its ability to help people contact the spirit world. Soon they discovered they had a lot in common. Pat decided that she and Steve could ask their questions together, because Ouija boards usually require two pairs of hands to function most effectively. It occurred to Steve that he might be able to construct a Ouija board for himself out of heavy cardboard, which he could letter with the alphabet, the words "Yes" and "No," one at each corner, and numerals zero through nine. He could use an old audio cassette box as the little pointer that came in Pat's game, and thus both would have a Ouija board. This is something you can do also, whether or not your toy store stocks this popular game.

Pat and Steve went to a quiet table in a picnic area nearby the toy store and began their readings. By this time Pat had told Steve all about Roger, how he was so unreliable and how she was ready to settle down but had doubts about whether Roger ever would make a commitment. Steve told Pat about his ex-girl friend Loretta, who ran out on him to marry his best friend and how now he felt a little shy about returning to the singles scene. Each provided the other with support and encouragement, and both were willing to try the Ouija board with an open mind—an essential ingredient.

The Ouija board works through a series of vibrations. The people who are placing their hands on the pointer seem to be moving it, but actually they are not. The proper way to achieve contact with the spirits around you is to reach inside yourself to allow them to make a connection with your higher self. Your higher self is the most powerful part of you—in fact, you are a small part of your higher self, not the other way around. Your higher self can then connect with the spirit world and let those who have information to impart speak through your body.

How is this done? First of all, you must have an attitude of trust and love. Saying a prayer at the outset is a good idea. Make something up yourself along these lines: "I release my ego to God. I am part of God, and God is part of me. I ask for clear guidance and accurate information, in so far as you can provide it and I may know it. Help me to be a clear channel." Then take a few deep breaths to relax yourself, just like you would for meditation. Picture a huge beacon of white light surrounding you—do this before attempting any psychic exercise. Always reach for the brightest light, because that is the purest, most spiritual energy. As you relax and take deep breaths, draw more and more of the light into your being until you have a sense that you are merging with the light. At that point you may even be able to hear voices. These are your spirit guides. As long as you get a positive feeling from this exercise, you are safe. If it ever begins to feel unsafe, negative, or potentially threatening, call for the light. Surround yourself with more light. You can even say out loud that you will tolerate no spirits who are not from the whitest of light. Then you will be safe.

Pat and Steve set up Pat's Ouija board on the table between them and proceeded to take the steps described above. When both were sufficiently relaxed and receptive, they each put a couple of fingers from each hand on the pointer with a pressure that was almost feather light. Steve indicated that Pat should go first, and so she asked whether they had made contact with a spirit who would answer their questions. The pointer slowly moved to "Yes." Both Pat and Steve smiled happily, but were a little astonished. Pat's next question was to ask the name of the spirit. That is a good first step, because not only is it good manners to introduce yourself to a companion—whether earthly or otherworldly—but you can also call on a spirit to return once you know its name. Pat and Steve concentrated and continued their slow, deep breathing as the pointer spelled out, letter by letter, the name "Arrowsmith."

Upon reading that name, and then saying it aloud, Pat sensed that she had a deep connection with Arrowsmith. She thanked the spirit for coming. Manners are always important, and those in the spirit world appreciate them even more than we on earth do. By then Pat felt totally comfortable and looked forward to getting answers that would set her mind at ease at last.

Her first question was about Roger and whether or not he was her soul mate. The pointer moved slowly, very slowly. Ouija boards demand great patience and concentration, for it is hard to maintain a strong connection with a spirit at first, and frequently those in spirit have a difficult time with spelling. Thus we must help them and try to understand as well as we can. Gradually the answer was clear: "You wouldn't have to ask." Pat and Steve thought about this for a while and began to see the meaning—if Roger were Pat's soul mate, she would know; she wouldn't have to ask. She then asked what her connection with Roger was. Once again, the pointer moved slowly. It spelled out the word love. Pat took a deep breath, believing that Arrowsmith was telling her that love was the basis of her relationship with Roger, and that was a cheery answer. But the pointer kept on moving. The second word it spelled out was practice. "Love practice." She and Steve had to laugh over this bit of information. Often spirits will be terse in their replies. But they are not trying to be cryptic, simply to be efficient and to save as much energy as possible so that they can be of maximum service.

Pat began to feel a sense of calm and understanding. A lot of the stress associated with her involvement with Roger had disappeared. Pat then began to wonder about her future. She voiced her feeling that she was ready to settle down, but if not with Roger, then with whom? And when would he come along? Was she ready to marry? It's okay to ask complicated, interwoven questions, for they help clarify matters to you as well as for the spirit, who can then go on to create an all-encompassing reply. That is what Arrowsmith did. The Ouija board spelled out a puzzling message—"There is no coincidence." What could that mean? Pat and Steve couldn't understand how that reply answered Pat's question about the future. They decided to mull it over while Steve took a turn asking his question. Of course we know the answer—Pat's meeting with Steve was no coincidence, because Steve is Pat's soul mate, something they will discover soon.

Steve asked first if Arrowsmith could answer some of his questions. Pat interjected that it might be best if a spirit connected with Steve took over. They asked if that were true. The pointer spelled out the word intermediary, implying that Arrowsmith could act as an intermediary for Steve. Obviously, Arrowsmith had the strongest connection with the two people and the Ouija board at that moment. Later, when Pat and Steve become more adept at channeling spirits, many other entities might come forth, some of them even more sophisticated than Arrowsmith.

They allowed Arrowsmith to continue, graciously saying thank you for the information received so far and all the spirit's hard work. Steve then asked why his girlfriend had run off with his best friend. The reply was "your good luck." Steve and Pat had a good chuckle over that one, realizing that not only had the spirit answered the question, but that Arrowsmith had made a joke as well. Steve's next question was about whether or not he was ready to have a happy romance. The pointer simply reached for the word "Yes". Steve and

Pat smiled at each other. Then Pat asked where Steve would meet his future lover. Slowly, laboriously, the pointer spelled out the phrase, "in the light." What could that mean? Once again Steve and Pat were baffled. They couldn't see how clear it was that they had met each other in the light—the light they had entered together to use the Ouija board.

Steve then decided to seek some deeper information. It had occurred to him that he and Pat were sharing an unusual rapport. They seemed to make eye contact that provided amazing depths of information. He asked Arrowsmith if he and Pat had any spiritual connection from either past lives or other means that would explain why they had bonded so easily. When Pat heard Steve's question, she recognized the truth of his statement and she learned something. When you meet a soul mate, the response and recognition are instantaneous. The answer shone out of her sparkling eyes almost immediately, an answer that Steve could read and answered with his own smile of joy. The pointer hesitated for a moment, then inched, letter by letter, on its journey of revelation. Eventually it spelled out, "Many lives. Many loves. Past. Present. Future." Arrowsmith was telling them what they had discovered in each other's eyes—they were soul mates who had once again found each other. Steve and Pat were incredibly moved by this information. They both felt joy, anticipation, and fear because of their failed past experiences.

Steve asked how they could assure that things would work out between them. This was a complicated question that required a complex reply. Finally the message was clear. "No guarantee. Your choice always. Moment by moment. Relax and live." As is fairly clear, Arrowsmith was warning them that there is never any guarantee in life, not even with lovers who have been together forever. Each moment is created anew by people who care and make individual choices each time. Pat and Steve should take their time and get to know each other—after all, they just met. Even if they are the best soul mates, they still have to discover each other's personalities, likes and dislikes in this lifetime. Arrowsmith wanted them to relax, not to use this information to create stress by pushing too fast or too hard for a relationship that they should develop gradually. There is no substitute for life, no matter how much insight we bring to any situation. Pat and Steve were both so excited and happy—and eager to go off together to talk so that they could get better acquainted—that they thanked Arrowsmith, packed up the game, and set off hand in hand.

Yes, this is an amazing story. Few people meet a soul mate as a result of a Ouija board. But we can learn about our soul mates as a result of using such a device. Just as Pat and Steve learned, the potential to receive vastly complicated and rewarding information is there. The point is to develop the proper receptivity first. Don't assume that it is easy, despite the fact that Ouija boards are sold as a game. They are one of the most difficult spiritual devices to use. That's not to say that anyone can't make the pointer spell out all sorts of words. Anyone can. The trick is in making the strongest possible connection to the spirit world and thereby to receive valid information, not merely the product of your own imagination. The way to do that is with hard work and with the help of a meditative state of mind.

Suppose you do achieve such a state of mind and

receive some messages from the Ouija board. How can you tell if it is accurate? You have to reach inside yourself and see if it feels right. If you have a deep feeling of peace and trust, then you have probably connected with a spirit, because these are the hallmarks of spiritual interaction. But if you have lots of nagging doubts, perhaps you have tricked yourself. This is the deepest problem faced by people who do psychic work. What if I have tricked myself? We all ask that question a thousand times. The best barometer of success is that when you have connected absolutely, you know it absolutely. There is no doubt. At other times you may be receiving a partial transference or even an answer that you have made up yourself.

What if you can't get the pointer to move at all? This is a distinct possibility, because it is hard to release control of your body to a spirit. The best solution in this matter is simply to keep trying. If you really want to do this, eventually you will. Just like anything else, spiritual work takes practice and determination. It also takes trust. Work on achieving your altered state of consciousness. Practice meditation—after all, that can benefit you in every area of your life. And believe that it is possible. You'll get it when you're ready for it. That is one of the essential laws of psychic work. When we're ready, it's easy—of course, after all that discipline and hard work, anything is easy!

Also remember to choose your partners carefully. A disbelieving partner who is pressed into service simply because he or she has the essential ingredients—two hands—is worse than no partner at all. Work only with people who are willing and believers. Ridicule or disinterest are not conducive to positive results.

It is possible to work the pointer on your own. You can also have more than one partner. In either case, it's just a matter of having the proper energy field accompanied by the right state of mind. With the right attitude you can learn a lot about yourself, your life, and those around you. Remember always to go slowly, to be open to the light, and not to put too much pressure on yourself or on the Ouija board. Also remember not to give the board all your power. If you abdicate all decisions to the Ouija board, your spirits will stop answering you. The purpose of all spiritual tools is to provide greater enlightenment and the ability to live your life with a greater degree of awareness, enhanced purpose, and new strength and individuality. Use yours as a tool to attain these things, and you will not only be better informed but happier.

CHAPTER VIII

Following your paths

BY NOW YOU HAVE PROBABLY BECOME quite an expert in the different areas covered by this book. If you have tried all the various techniques, then you have a good sense about what the future holds for you and your love life. You may also have discovered something else—that you find some techniques easier than others, that you receive what seem like more appropriate answers from the methods you favor. This is perfectly natural. There are many areas of the occult, and each is designed to give insight and information, but not each area is equally easy to master. Just as a town may have many roads leading to Main Street, the occult has many paths—all leading to the same essential truths. Follow the ones you're most comfortable with.

Once you get over your initial amazement at discovering how incredibly accurate each technique is, you are prepared to go on and to use the information you have received. If all signs are telling you to take a certain tack in your romance, pay attention! This is your chance to use this valuable information to make your love life just what you want it to be. That way you'll be more in charge of your own destiny than ever and you'll have the chance to find all the happiness you desire and deserve. Good luck!

ABOUT THE AUTHOR

NANCY FREDERICK SUSSAN is an astrologer who writes about a variety of metaphysical topics. Her articles appear frequently in every astrology magazine on the stands. She is the editor of ASTRO SIGNS, read daily by upwards of half a million people across the U.S. and Canada. Ms. Sussan recently relocated from New York to beautiful Los Angeles, where she writes, teaches astrology, and counsels a large private clientele.

In your quest for true love, let the heavens help you!
Lynx Books presents

the love life guides

#1 *Starring Your Love Life:* An astrological guide to finding true love.

#2 *It all Adds Up to Love:* Numerology provides great insight into the most important numbers in life and love.

#3 *The Lover's Dream:* Learn to interpret and reprogram your dreams to find the perfect mate.

#4 *Tarot: Love is in the Cards:* Unveil the mystery of the Tarot and stack the deck in your favor for love!

#5 *Palmistry: All Lines Lead to Love:* Learn to read your own—or your lover's—palm to discover your romantic potential.

#6 *Love Games: Psychic Paths to Love:* A variety of New Age means to finding romance.